LARK
ASCENDING

ALSO BY SILAS HOUSE:

Clay's Quilt

A Parchment of Leaves

The Coal Tattoo

The Hurting Part

Eli the Good

Something's Rising:
Appalachians Fighting Mountaintop Removal,
with Jason Kyle Howard

Same Sun Here, with Neela Vaswani

Southernmost

LARK
ASCENDING

A NOVEL BY

SILAS HOUSE

ALGONQUIN BOOKS
OF CHAPEL HILL 2022

Published by
ALGONQUIN BOOKS OF CHAPEL HILL
Post Office Box 2225
Chapel Hill, North Carolina 27515-2225

an imprint of
WORKMAN PUBLISHING CO. INC.
a subsidiary of
HACHETTE BOOK GROUP, INC.
1290 Avenue of the Americas
New York, NY 10104

LIBRARY OF CONGRESS CATALOGING-IN-PUBLICATION DATA

[Names: House, Silas, [date]– author.
Title: Lark ascending : a novel / by Silas House.
Description: First Edition. | Chapel Hill, North Carolina : Algonquin Books
of Chapel Hill, 2022. | Summary: "In the near future, as fires devastate most
of the United States, Lark and his family secure a place on a boat headed to
Ireland, which is rumored to be accepting refugees and is the last country not
yet overrun by extremists"— Provided by publisher.
Identifiers: LCCN 2022016100 | ISBN 9781643751597 (hardcover) |
ISBN 9781643753447 (ebook)
Subjects: LCGFT: Novels.
Classification: LCC PS3558.O8659 L37 2022 | DDC 813/.54—dc23
LC record available at https://lccn.loc.gov/2022016100

10 9 8 7 6 5 4 3 2 1
First Edition

This book is for Joy Harris.

In a dark time
the eye begins to see.

—THEODORE ROETHKE

LARK
ASCENDING

1

LARK

THEY HAVE ALL asked me to write down the whole particulars about how I came to be here, from the beginning to the end, keeping nothing back. So now, in my old age, I need to begin with our journey, when my parents and I crossed the wide Atlantic in the hopes of sanctuary on the green island of Ireland. Eventually I will need to go further back to make everything clear, but this is the real beginning, because it is when I knew I had to take control of the journey and when I had to make the decision if I would live or die.

What I recall best is the noise.

The thrashing of heavy sprays, the thundering of the sails, the shrill cries of the crew. The suffering of the seasick. I was ill the entire first week of the crossing. Most everyone was, all of us hanging off the sides of the boat, moaning and retching. Worst of all, though, was that for days there was only the dry heaving, so bad my stomach must have bruised from the violence of it all. Even after the worst passed, I lay between sleep and waking, my eyes wide open in the darkness, the sickness gone but replaced by my head swimming and my body giddying, which was almost worse to bear. Just the thought of those days makes my stomach churn again.

I've never known such misery, despite what I've been through since. I have had many adventures in my life but there is no matching that anguished time. There's pain and suffering, and then there is misery, which is what we lived while we crossed the ocean. And of course, none of us was as bad off as my father, although I wouldn't realize that for many days into the voyage.

My mother worked with the crew the entire time. There was always something to do with the sails, and although she had never been on a sailboat, she got the hang of it better than the rest of the ragtag crew. Everyone on that six-person crew barely slept. If they got sick, they worked through it. Most of them had wormed their way onto the boat promising to work in trade for the passage over. The *Covenant* had once been a grand yacht meant to carry about ten wealthy passengers. The boat was most likely stolen from some unwatched dock in the wake of the war. Now it was scraped and worn but still sturdy, with two large sails latched to thick masts.

"Pay attention!" the captain yelled at least once a day when she felt the crew was not adjusting the sails quickly enough. She was a giant of a woman who was always angry and anxious. She had no teeth, which made her face seem thinner and meaner. Then, quietly but with even more frustration, to herself: "That is the most important thing." After which she would close her eyes and make her lips move in prayer. To what force I don't know. The ocean, most likely, as it controlled her entire world.

I watched the captain all the time because I watched everyone. That was the only way I remained sane, but it is also just how I have always been. My father used to say I noticed things that others did not and for that reason I might be an artist someday. But that was before everything happened, before we were just trying to keep ourselves alive hour by hour.

That first week my father did little more than care for me, although he was in far worse shape than I was and besides, I was twenty years old and I had seen most of the people I cherished die in front of me. So I was grown in every way a person can be. But there I was, accordioned across my father's arms, helpless, as our boat rose and fell across the dark blue sea. There was not much he could do, anyway, nothing more than lie there beside me. I didn't realize it at the time but the injuries to his leg were already working on his mind, as well. This truth would present itself soon enough.

Sometimes I heard the others on the boat making fun of me—*someone that useless ought to throw himself overboard*—but I wasn't just seasick; I was undone in sorrow. Only days before, we had been a family of six, and now we were only three. Every time I retched over the side of the boat, I felt like I was vomiting up some of that grief. But nothing can get that out of you, no matter how hard you try. I did find that something as simple as my father rubbing my back in a perfect circle during the worst bouts at least calmed me a little. Sometimes I lay against him as if I were a child again and he cooed against my ear and that helped, too. Everyone else on that boat was going through the same thing in one way or another. Grief had ravaged us all. We were the survivors, and we all had lived through nightmare days. I thought I was at my lowest place, but I didn't know that things would soon get worse.

By the end of that first week, I stood and got back to work. We had witnessed most of the country burning and what followed: the food shortages, the war, the migrations. We had lived just fine on our own for seven years up in the mountains, surviving seven brutal winters in those Maine woods. We had buried people we loved, with our own hands. We had walked all the way to Nova Scotia, risking everything so we could catch this boat. We were survivors. And we were going to make it across this ocean.

THE RAIN PUMMELED us for four straight days and caused the crew—mostly my mother—to never stop pulling at ropes and adjusting sails. During those days she must not have slept more than a couple of hours a night, when I relieved her. This only happened when the winds died down enough for me to handle the lines. And a couple times there was even a calm spell when we drifted along and I could close my eyes, imagining myself back home in Maine, on the mountain, the only place I had ever been safe in my whole life. In those interludes there was nothing but the sound of the water slapping against the boat. Everyone was either asleep or silent in their misery and there would be a kind of peace for a time. I'd open my eyes and look out at the aching blue of the ocean—a color I had never seen in nature and that most likely only exists in the middle of the Atlantic, a gray blue like a storm cloud full of unspent lightning and unfallen rain. There was some comfort in knowing that, although the world was being torn in two, there were still remarkable things that went on being, that refused to lose their shine. Some days it was only the wonder that kept us going.

But then, one morning the sun stained the far horizon a rich pink that made everyone feel better. One of the old women said the sky was the color of grapefruit meat, but I was too young to have ever seen such a thing, and this meant little more than to remind me that there had been a whole world before that one generation could recall vividly while another could not conjure it at all. For an entire week after that pink-like-no-other-pink, we had smooth sailing weather.

We had not known how small the refugee boat was
when we gave nearly everything we had to board it, but
we would have had no choice either way. Since the captain
liked to recite these facts on occasion, I learned that the
Covenant had been intended for the calmer coastal waters
around America and now she would have to cross the wide
Atlantic. She was forty-three meters in length—about 140
feet. There were forty-four of us in the beginning. There
was not one moment for twenty-seven days that I wasn't
up against at least three people at once. There was so little
space that we had no choice but to lie upon one another. By
the seventh day four people had jumped overboard, driven
mad by the lack of room. I tried to not think about what
happened to them. Which would be worse—to drown and
drift down to the darkest depths of the ocean or to be eaten
by sharks and shat out into the sea?

The first death aboard was a man who died of a heart
attack, and we all gathered to pay our respects and lift his
body over the edge of the boat to drop it into the sea. He
had been one of the men who had helped me get my father
aboard on that first day, his gray eyes steady on mine as
I made that step from certain death to the thrill of hope.
Miriam, who was brave enough to reveal that she was a
priest and had managed to hide from the Slaughters, said
the rites, which she still knew by heart. The dead man was
large, and I was surprised by what a small sound he made,
being swallowed by the water.

For a while, there was a baby who cried throughout each night. Every time the crying stopped—just as dawn began to light the wide ocean—I was sure the baby boy had died of whatever ailment caused him to wail, but within minutes shrieks began again. The wailing was the loudest when darkness crept in with its purpling and then graying ways. I never saw the infant. Not once. The baby and his mother were on the other end of the boat, and in the daytime, she kept the sleeping tyrant tucked beneath her blouse to keep the sun from roasting his skin. The baby died on the ninth day, and when we bowed our heads to acknowledge his passing and dropped his small bundle into the ocean, his sound was no smaller than the large man's had been. I couldn't help feeling thankful—I was glad for an end to the baby's endless protests, I'll admit, but mostly because we all knew there was nothing but misery awaiting him anyway. And despite our sadness, the silence his absence provided was a wonder. I had expected the infant's mother to take up wailing where her child had left off, but until the day she died, she sat looking out on the ocean as if shaping her own face into a tombstone.

From the beginning my mother argued with the captain, especially after my father folded himself up, overtaken by the pain he could no longer bear. He was the strongest man I had ever known, but lying there for days with a dying leg had taken everything from him.

"He's supposed to be a doctor!" the captain yelled at my mother. "All he does is sit and stare off into space."

"If you knew how to control your boat, he wouldn't have been caught between it and the raft motor," my mother said, her voice as calm as if she were introducing herself. She was taking a gamble that the captain would not actually check in on my father, because he had not been harmed by any fault of the boat as my mother was claiming. The truth was, a knife had been plunged into his leg a week before we boarded, and blood poisoning was slithering its way through his body. "Do you expect him to tend to the sick on a crushed leg?"

So she and I had to work twice as hard to make up for my father's inability. And she had to give a portion of the seeds to the captain or be thrown overboard. Before the deal was struck, there had been much shouting about this and the captain had two of the crew grab my mother by the arms, hustling her toward the side of the boat.

I rushed forward, ready to fight them all in an attempt to save her. By this point the pain and sepsis had taken my father to somewhere in his mind where he didn't even have the ability to flinch at the possibility of his wife being murdered.

Another two of the crew members held me back as I screamed and kicked at air. We all reeked at that point but one of them stank so badly—a slick scent of unwashed genitals and dirty hair—that I gagged at the smell of him, even in my rage.

There was a whole group of people—led by Miriam—who locked arms and stood in front of the captain. "We won't sit by while you commit murder," Miriam said, her eyes hard and blue gray as the sea. "We won't allow it. She and her son are doing all they can."

The captain looked to Miriam as if she might reply, but then her gaze went out over the ocean. She stood thinking for a time, her square fists planted on her tremendous hips, while I struggled against the men. My mother made no movement there on the edge of the boat and it seemed that she was preparing herself to die. Just when I thought they might actually shove her into the ocean, there was a deal made about the seeds.

At last, the captain spat a gelatinous wad into the sea and nodded her chin to the men holding my mother. "Let her go," she said. "For now."

And from then on everyone on the boat knew my mother was a seed-saver, so we had to watch ourselves even more than before. We had always slept in shifts but now when it was my turn to keep watch, I never took my hand off the knife that hung in a leather pouch around my neck. Now my eyes scanned back and forth over the rocking boat, always expecting someone to rob us.

SOMETIMES AS THE gloaming crept toward us over the ocean, the little children gathered around Miriam while she sang very old songs from the Before:

You belong among the wildflowers

or

I can't live, with or without you

or

Never mind, I'll find someone like you

Her voice was deep and rich and no matter what she sang, everything sounded mournful and full of longing. Every song made me think of Arlo. Made me think of the three graves we had left behind us that day in those woods.

On the eleventh day my father's panics started.

He was unable to catch his breath. At first he calmed down if I did just what he had done for me during my lowest point: whisper *Shhh, shhh* into his ear and rub his back in a perfect circle.

But the attacks grew worse. On the thirteenth day, he clawed at his chest and his eyes rolled back in his head.

"Daddy," I whispered, something I had not called him in years. Our plan all along was to draw as little attention to ourselves as we could and now the entire boat not only knew we were seed-savers but also that my father was screaming and thrashing. We had everyone's attention. On the other side of the boat my mother kept steady, tightening the sails while the other crew members slurped down their daily ration of canned beans. "Calm down, it's okay."

He rubbed at his heart with the tips of his fingers.

"Look, the water is nice, the sky's clear," I pleaded. "Just hold on and we'll be okay. We're fine."

But I knew that we were not. I knew that we had never been worse.

Mostly he looked at me with tears brimming in his eyes, staring at me as if he was trying to tell me something but could not put it into words.

His whole body trembled, shaking uncontrollably. His lips, his hands, his head, his poisoned leg. Seeing him with no control over his own body hurt me worse than any of it.

"My heart," he stammered, quietly at first, but then, with each word building into a frantic scream: "My heart's. Beating. Out of. MY! CHEST!"

That brought my mother to us. She took his face in her hands and kissed him with her cracked, wind-burned lips on the forehead, on each eye, on the mouth. "Stay with us, my darling," she said. She was not the kind of person who revealed herself but in this moment her voice was full of pain. "Come on, now, my darling. Please."

She turned and dug frantically in the one pack we had, which contained everything we owned, the duffel bag we protected at all costs. Her hands shook. We were nearing the end. I can barely stand to remember the way she looked at him, beseeching him to come back to her. She wedged open his crusted lips and shook a spoonful of turmeric onto his teeth, then forced his mouth shut. "It's all I have left for the pain," she whispered to me, but kept her eyes on his face.

There was a quiet woman whose name I never knew, with a quiet child called Charlotte. They always kept near us, as if they had some sense that we were safer people than others on the boat. They both slept on the other side of my mother. On that day the woman approached my father and held his hand as if they had known each other a long time. "Never mind," she repeated several times, in low coos. Eventually the repetition of this strange phrase calmed him into a steady breathing. For a time.

On the fifteenth day he became delusional.

"Take the knife and cut them off," he said, over and over until I could not bear to hear it. His arm shot out and took hold of the knife I kept around my neck, pulling it so hard that I was propelled forward, but wrestling it away from him wasn't difficult. "The devil has ahold of my legs and won't let go. Take the knife and—" I capped my hands over my ears and hummed—*This one goes out to the one I love*—to block out his cries. I had never heard him speak of anything such as the devil before. I had surely never heard him cry out like this. Then I lost my patience and pressed my hand over his mouth so he would stop. I'm haunted by how it must have hurt when I pushed his blistered lips against his teeth. But perhaps this was a brief distraction from the poison coursing through his veins. Still, I have so many regrets such as this. That is the thing people rarely mention to you about grief: all of the regrets.

Sometimes he whispered this same thing over and over—*cut them off, cut them*—even when he slept, or had some semblance of sleep.

Even though the nights were icy, he broke out in full body sweats that caused our clothes to be drenched as we held on to him. He thought he was choking to death and clawed at his throat until his fingernails left bloody lines up and down his neck.

"Daddy," I whispered over and over again. This was the only word of comfort I had for him, but looking back I realize that this word offered comfort to me more than anyone.

And then, on the twentieth day, I had been in the deepest sleep I could ever recall. A sleep like being under the ocean, like being back in my mother's womb. A sleep like death must feel. But even in this profound rest I was aware of something not quite right, and coming awake felt like swimming up from far down in the water, my eyes latched onto a dim light just above the surface. I pulled my arms through the water, heavy as thick mud. As I struggled to full wakefulness, I felt that quick rush of concern one feels just before they've broken through the waves to draw in a deep breath.

Then I heard the same small sound the large man had made when they gave his body to the Atlantic. The same small sound the baby had made when it was dropped into the sea. Only this time I knew that the sound was the last utterance of my father. He was no longer beside me, and he had not left that spot since we had climbed onto this boat and dragged him over the side, despite the protests of so many who said we should have left him behind. He'd be of no use now with the damaged leg, they'd said. That's just the way it is, one of them said. And so my mother had struck the deal with the captain. But now he had given himself to the sea.

I felt I had become paralyzed in my sleep. I could hear and see but that was all. I knew my father was dead. He had sacrificed himself for us, to rid us of his burden. I knew he had pulled himself and his lifeless legs overboard in the night, but I couldn't tell anyone. I was unable to dive in after him.

I saw him as he had once been: swinging the red-bladed axe over his head to cut wood for our cabin, cupping his hands into the icy water of the creek and drawing a drink up to his mouth, strolling out of the woods with a rabbit hanging from his belt. I saw him throw back his head to laugh, saw him take hold of my mother's hand as they walked down the path in front of me, saw him reciting a poem as we sat around the fire together at night. There he was, leaning down to kiss Arlo's forehead just before we buried him. There he was, running through the creek and screaming for me to run, too.

Only rarely in the night was my mother with us because she crewed all day, and often all night, too. But that night she had fallen, exhausted, between me and the child, Charlotte, who had curved in around her for warmth. In my slow-motion state, I turned my head and there she was, sound asleep. My father had been in that small space between us and now he was gone forever.

The starlight was plentiful. I could see my mother and all of the other people even though it was the very middle of the night. The ocean sounded different at this hour. Even the sails possessed a different timbre. The click of the stays, the *flomp flomp* of loose ropes. Everyone was asleep except for the crew, who were silent. All of the bodies around me were lit by a wash of silver from the stars. I struggled to move but I knew there was no use. I knew that he was gone, plunging toward the bottom of the ocean like a slender knife. I imagined him, arms out, toes pointed, free at last. I latched my eyes onto the sky, thinking of a song he had sung to me when I was little.

When the stars go blue.

Then I was able to move. I brought my hand up as if lifting a boulder and managed to nudge my mother's shoulder. Her eyes opened right away, calmly. As if she had been waiting for me, as if she already knew.

FOR DAYS I watched the dark blue water as if my father might emerge from the waves and put his hand out to be pulled back in, his legs healed by the saltwater. My sickness returned, but this time I didn't think it was the constant rise and fall of the ocean so much as my hopelessness that caused me to throw up until the dry heaves racked my body.

The captain grabbed hold of my shoulders. "Get to work or follow your father," she said, her wide face near mine. Up close like that I could see a constellation of freckles across her nose that made her face less hard. I didn't hate her. I didn't feel anything. I took my shift running the ropes and found that being up and about helped to settle my stomach. Many hours later the captain appeared behind me. "You did good," she whispered, as if afraid someone else might witness her small kindness. "Go on and try to rest now."

Many days passed before my mother spoke to me. "Lark, we have to keep going," she said. In a way this made no sense because I *was* going. I had been working the ropes for the last ten hours on my own. The work was more comforting than stillness. But in another way she knew that I was giving up.

I saw that she had changed completely in the last couple of days. New lines striped her forehead. Her eyes were sunken, her high cheekbones more prominent. I knew she had been starving herself so my father and I would have more to eat. For a week now we'd had nothing more each day than one can of beans to split between the three of us. At some point in the hours after his death I'd had the sick thought that at least we'd have a little more food now. I couldn't stand that I had allowed that to slither through my mind. I pictured it, shimmering like an electric eel. Something black-eyed and ruthless. Something made completely of hunger. I am an old man now, propped here on what I believe will be my deathbed, and I still bear the guilt for this thought. My mother's lips were so chapped they were bleeding in small places. They were moving. She was talking, but all I heard was the wind. The never-ending eternal ceaseless sound of the ocean. That was the sound of eternity: the wind.

"Don't give up, Lark," she was saying, when I managed to hear her again. I thought to myself that I ought to memorize her. Burn her into my mind's eye. Her ears had been crisply sunburned even though most days there had been only low gray skies. Her hair was wild and matted. "We can't. Do you hear me?"

I nodded. *Don't give up*, I wanted to reassure her, but I was unable to even whisper these three words. I said them only in my mind. *Don't give up*. A perfect short prayer.

My mother pointed into the air now. "Look at that," she said. Above us greenish-blue clouds were roiling together with such ferocity that I thought we might be able to hear them groaning if not for the noise of the wind. She had told me once that green clouds meant that land was nearby. "We'll still have to get around to the eastern side of Ireland, but we're so close, Lark. If we can just make it through this storm, by tomorrow we'll see land."

The thought of solid ground felt impossible now, but the mention of the word *land* caused hope to bloom in my chest like the moment when dry leaves take the flame and spring into fire. I nodded again, this time with more emphasis, and something stirred in me that made me feel less dead.

"But the storm's going to wreak havoc. You have to watch the lines like you never have before."

"I'm not good at it," I said.

"Just do what the captain tells you and you'll do fine."

Nighttime hunkered over us and still the storm did not come. Yet we could feel it building above us, boiling and churning. *Around* us.

Far away over the ocean we could see lightning moving toward us until finally the white foam at the tops of the growing waves was illuminated. But still the rain did not come.

The waves grew larger and larger until finally one giant rolling toward us was revealed by a long stretch of lightning. A deafening peal of thunder chased along at the heels of the flash.

The wave came straight at us. We all held on to one another or anything we could find to grab. I clutched only the lines. I kept my eye on the sails, listening carefully to my mother's screamed instructions. The captain stood at the stern of the ship, hollering as she tried to steer. I barely even registered it when I saw her swept overboard. I was numb from feeling anything when I saw one, two, then five, then seven people, thrust into the sea.

The boat canted and bucked while the spray flew in every direction.

I felt myself sailing through the air and thought I had been thrown from the pitching boat before I realized that my mother had grabbed me. She latched an orange life vest around my chest and then we were both hurled onto the wooden floor. My head hit hard enough for me to see brief stars. She lay atop me, holding on to the mast. Saltwater ran into my eyes and mouth, the iciness of it sending a scream through my whole body. The noise around us was overwhelming. Ocean and thunder and yelling and ocean, ocean. The silver sound of the wind.

I felt the entire boat swing upward, standing on its side at a complete ninety-degree angle. All around me people were letting go, falling into the water.

There was a sickening crunch as one of the two masts broke in two, then the quake as it fell onto the boat and crushed several beneath its weight before tumbling off into the sea.

But then I realized we had not flipped over, that the *Covenant* had miraculously righted herself again and was bobbing on the ocean, crippled but intact except for the lost mast, which would cut our horsepower in half.

My mother lay atop me and held on to the bottom of the remaining mast with all of her might, keeping us both from being thrown overboard, protecting me from the pounding rain—I could hear it now, like stones pummeling us—and from the lightning.

After a while she rolled onto the floor beside me, panting for breath. I could hear the storm moving out and away over the ocean, lifting its skirts for speed, leaving us behind. She had saved me, once again. Just as she had before. Just as my father had done before, too. But now he was gone and it was only the two of us in the wide world, with not one other person alive who cared if we lived or died. Above us there was nothing but a night sky of churning clouds, and somewhere behind their denseness were the stars going blue. But I couldn't look long because tiny needles of rain stung my eyes.

MORNING. WHITE LIGHT. Calm waters. The peaceful sound of the ocean nipping sweetly at the boat.

Above me: a clear sky. Once there was a bluish-purple flower in the Maine woods my mother had shown me. *Anemone*, she had said, sliding the stem between two fingers so she could cup it in her hand without picking the bloom. I loved the word and used to repeat it to myself when I tried to go to sleep. I had not thought of that in a long while. But that morning I did, because the sky was anemone blue.

I said the word aloud. Four syllables, four prayers. To the sky, to the word itself, to the flower.

And birds. Gulls. We had not seen any birds in ages. Here was an entire flock, crying out and wheeling, caught up in a frantic gossip as if they had missed seeing people.

My mother slept the sleep of pure exhaustion beside me. I rose up, amazed by the sight of the birds. I didn't know how she could have slept through their clamor. I nudged her and didn't take my eyes away from gulls. "Birds," I said, feeling like that was the only word I could conjure.

She sat up and put a hand to her brow. "Ireland," she breathed out, even though there was nothing but miles of ocean before us. "The birds mean we're close."

Of the forty-four of us when we'd left America, there were now nineteen, seven of those children. That's when I noticed Charlotte standing all by herself. I recognized the slack look that had overtaken her face. Malnutrition, first and foremost. But shock, too. I put my hand out and she came over to me without changing her expression.

"She's gone," she said, talking about her mother, the quiet woman. Charlotte was maybe ten years old, a small pale moth of a child.

"You stay close to me, all right?"

She nodded, once.

All of us gathered together to discuss what we'd do when we got near Ireland. We had made it, unlike so many others before us.

"We will surrender the boat to them as soon as we get close," my mother said. "And remember that they'll probably take us to a refugee camp to quarantine for a while, so don't be frightened."

"Remember: don't resist, don't talk back," Miriam told

us, all of the children except Charlotte huddled in close to her. Miriam was holding on to two of them, one on either side. "Just put your arms out to be zip-tied."

Some of the children began to cry at that. I realized that all of them were now orphaned.

The crewman called Hogan, a hunched, stinking man with only a ring of stringy hair, had been one of those who had held my mother and had been ready to push her from the boat at the captain's order. I had seen that he had been disappointed when a deal was struck and she'd walked away. Now he spoke. "Better to go to an Irish refugee camp than to die back home in the fires."

This didn't comfort the children any.

Charlotte did not cry but she did grab hold of my shirt-tail and step closer.

"It'll be slow going but the remaining mainsail will carry us in," my mother said. She had taken over for the captain since no one else had stepped up to do so.

We had some canned food left as it had been the most secured of all of our cargo during the storms. We would divide that; perhaps it would come in handy with the soldiers.

"I'll trade the last of the seeds to get us into the same camp," my mother whispered to me as she rummaged around in our duffel, seeing what we could possibly get rid of to make room for a few cans of beans. "We'll just use whatever we can to barter ourselves into our best chances."

"And Charlotte, too," I said.

She looked up at me as if she had not even realized that Charlotte was hovering in my shadow, striving to remain standing in her grief. Her eyes went from my face, to Charlotte, and back to me. "Lark—"

"We have to help her."

"It'll be hard enough for the two of us—"

"But we have to try," I said.

She kept her eyes on mine for a moment more and nodded.

We first saw land as twilight whispered itself into being. First there was the strange smudge on the horizon. Then shape. After a time, we thought that our eyes were conjuring land, but the closer we got, the greener the island became, until it was glowing green. Closer and we could see the high cliffs through our binoculars.

The *Covenant* plowed a straight line through the infinite ocean as she made her way toward land. As the sunset stained the western horizon we could see more: three small islands off to the right, a very white lighthouse standing on one of the high bluffs. A scattering of houses over there, close to the shore. No people anywhere.

About a mile out there came the sound waves, which caused us all to cower in place, clutching our heads between our hands. The pain was excruciating, causing a tremor through our muscles and bones. A buzz set up residence in my teeth that would not leave for a couple of days. Then, even worse, there was a huge explosion in the water near us. Fire and water tangled together and shot into the sky next to the boat.

Then: the *nip nip nip* of the bullets singing through the air all around us, immediately accompanied by screams and high cries.

I picked up Charlotte and she latched her small legs around my waist, her fingers sinking into my shoulders. She buried her face in the hollow place of my neck. "It's all right," I said, even though it clearly was not. "Don't be scared."

There were mines in the water and each time the boat drifted near there was another explosion. Then that low, unmistakable thud of the sound cannon and two seconds later the sound waves washed over us, bringing most of us to our knees with its particular pain, a kind of electricity that courses through your skin and bones and muscles and organs.

My mother was scrambling to get up and I expected her to go into action. Perhaps there were guns somewhere on the boat. A way to fight back. But she only grabbed hold of me. She pulled me to her and then held me by both wrists as she talked.

"They must've closed their borders, too many refugees," she said. "So they're shooting at us."

"They're shooting at us," I said, stupidly. But I couldn't believe it, after all it had taken for us to get here. They were supposed to take in anyone who made it.

"Things have changed since we left America," she said. "I think they mean to sink us."

She tightened my life vest, then ran to the cabinet and put hers on as she ran back to secure the other around the little girl. All around us people were jumping from the boat. That was the last thing I wanted to do.

"Listen to me," she said, and dug her thumbs deep into my chest as she took hold of my shoulders. "We have to get off of here."

I was amazed they'd fire on a boat full of people. "They're shooting—"

"Lark," Charlotte said, her voice quiet but full of panic. She was clinging to my arm now.

"If we get separated, just go to Glendalough," my mother said. I was taking in everything at once, so she grabbed hold of my chin to look at her. "It'll be four days' walk at the least, northeast."

Then I saw why everyone was jumping, many of them without life vests: the boat was sinking.

"Lark," she said, loudly. "Look at me."

I did. There was not so much fear on her face as determination. "If something happens to me. Don't give up."

I nodded, which in looking back was an odd thing to do. I should have embraced her, held on to her, said we'd never get separated, told her what she meant to me. But there's never time for that when you need it. All around us, bombs were exploding and gunfire was biting into the boat, and the sound waves kept coming.

"Try your best to not let go of my hand," my mother said, and I brought my free hand up to reassure myself that my knife was still around my neck as I said the same to Charlotte. Before I had time to tell my mother to wait, that her life vest wasn't latched, she jerked us along behind her, and before I knew what was happening we were jumping, falling, the wind sweeping over us, the churning ocean rushing up to meet us. The long drop sliced up through my belly, but before I had time to yell, I went under and the water was so cold it caused me to draw in my fill of the ocean just as I felt my mother's and Charlotte's fingers slip out of mine. I came up spitting and coughing among waves that were much larger than they had seemed from the boat. A big wave overtook me again, bringing full blindness. The life vest brought me back up but didn't keep me from being dragged under again and again. I was swallowing so much of the briny sea that I thought I might die there.

But when the life vest brought me bobbing to the surface again, I saw Charlotte swept backward, carried away by a wave, coughing up seawater with her eyes latched right on mine. She was pulling at her life vest as if trying to get it off. I screamed her name and swam toward her but it was no use, and even as I swam, I knew I'd never be able to get to her.

My mother was nowhere to be seen and I feared that one of the empty life vests bobbing on the waves had come off of her when we hit the water. I swam as hard as I could to get away from the pull of the boat, which was sinking faster now, letting out a great groan. I felt as if I was moving in place. All around me people were struggling to stay afloat or buoyed up by their life vests, some of them bloodied, others unconscious, others given up. I could see Miriam, clinging to a jagged chunk of the boat as two children with life vests clutched at her back, trying to climb up onto her as if she were a raft. Then I saw that Miriam wasn't clinging to the fiberglass. She was lying sprawled across it with a clean gunshot hole in place of her right eye. Miriam, who'd sung for us and had stood up for my mother.

A few yards from me I spotted my mother struggling to stay afloat, and I swam toward her. I don't know how she had managed the rough waters that long without a life vest or without holding on to something. I had never seen such a look of terror on her face before. That is the way I often remember her the most clearly. Just as I dove toward her, bullets pocked the water between us. Behind her, a massive plume of fire and water exploded, and she propelled herself underwater to escape this wrath.

She didn't come back up.

ψ ψ ψ

I SWAM AGAINST the heavy water, kicking and splashing. I felt as if I was moving through cement, until I was completely out of breath, and then I lay back and let the life vest and the current carry me. Somehow it took me away from the gunfire, out of the sight of the black drones swooping above the sea like large metal hornets.

Somehow, I was saved.

The ocean here was much calmer and I put distance between myself and the drones by swimming carefully toward shore. All I could think about was what might be below my feet. I had never been in the ocean before and imagined sharks teeming nearby, arguing over who might have the first bite of me. I made myself think only of getting ashore. The night sky was a rosy gray, just dark enough to reveal a slice of moon, as dark as it got this far north this time of year. I could see nothing but sandy bluffs and black boulders and a tangle of brush and vines. But it was dry land, which I had truly thought I might never set foot upon again. When at last the water became so shallow that I could walk ashore, I didn't know if I could make my legs move properly. It had been so long since I had stood on solid ground.

I climbed up onto the rocky beach within a horse-shoe-shaped cove. I was beyond cold, in a strange state where I felt both numb and in pain. I knew I had to get out of the water and get warm. My bones ached with the cold. One of my feet had gone numb, so I half ran, half dragged myself onto dry land. There was a melting path carved into the side of the high grassy bluff before me, and the water had worn a kind of dirt cave into its side where I could hide. The main thing was that I had to get warm.

But I knew the soldiers were nearby, so I'd be best suited to hide, yet there was certainly no way to build a fire without being spotted. They'd be making sure they got all of us. I realized the air was far warmer than the water had been, so I stripped off my clothes and arranged them on the rocks around me. Maybe enough sun would come out in the morning to dry them. I rubbed at my arms and legs and chest, and with a jagged bolt that felt like sickness in the pit of my belly, I realized that my leather pouch holding my knife had slipped over my head in the water. My last hope.

I curled up against the sharp black rocks at the back of the little cavern, waiting. I waited for hours, until the day bloomed and eased itself over the sea.

An entire day I lay there, exhausted, and maybe even past caring. I gave up for a time.

Each time I began to think about my mother and what had happened to her—shot? drowned?—I focused instead on how cold and miserable I was or how I had not eaten in almost two days and hadn't had a drink of water in hours and hours. My head pounded from the dehydration. Yet there was no pushing the grief away, and I admit that I allowed myself to have a fit of quiet crying for a time. I tried to convince myself that she had survived somehow but I knew that she was gone, down to those cold depths, and that's all there was to it. Gone like my father, like Arlo and Sera, like quiet little Charlotte, like everybody I had known my entire life. I was the last one of my people. Perhaps I was the last, period. Maybe everyone on that boat had died except for me. Maybe every single person back home was gone now, too. I had no way of knowing.

I was no stranger to death. I had seen it happen many times. But losing your parents is different. And being the only one left behind. To be alone like that is a grief all its own. I had been the only one left to take care of Charlotte and now I couldn't even do that. It was my fault she was dead. I eased out to the mouth of the cave and lay with the damp grit of sand against my face. I kept my eyes on the

Atlantic throughout the daylight, and there was not one speck of our boat left. No Charlotte waiting for me to come to her. No one was left.

Those with life vests should have been easy to spot out there in that glowing orange fabric, so easy that they had been picked up by the soldiers and carried off to the camps. Either way, they'd be dead soon, either starved or diseased. They were gone. We had all lived and suffered together for those nearly four weeks, so it was impossible to not feel something for them. Miriam, praying over the dead bodies. Charlotte's quiet mother sleeping beside us. The captain, unable to do anything except concentrate on making sure we survived. All gone. I thought of the way Charlotte had held on to me on the boat. I had been the most important person in the world for her although we had never spoken more than a dozen words to each other. Hardship has a way of bonding you to people, outside of anything you say to each other.

It would not have been difficult at all to become still there on that beach and let the thirst take me or run out into the opening and find the soldiers. It would have been so easy to wade back in and let the ocean swallow me. I could just allow the waves to carry me out until I was unable to swim back, down into the depths to hear the sound of for-ever in my ears as I died. But my mother had told me to not give up, and before her, my father had told me the same, and that's what I was going to do.

Glendalough. The one place that had given them hope. That is where I had to go, because when you have lost everything, you find something else to keep you going.

I woke the next morning to find my clothes still damp. I crept carefully up the narrow path that had been cut into the grassy slope, staying close to the ground, listening like an animal does, the way my parents had taught me. I heard nothing but the sea, that endless sound that will be the last sound when time is no more. I found an armload of twigs and small branches for kindling and one massive chunk of driftwood that would smolder awhile. There was a thin branch in the back of the cave that was dry enough for friction, but it must have taken a good hour before the flames took. My hands blistered from trying to make the sparks.

Once I had a little fire going, I tamped it down, so as not to give too much light, and dragged the driftwood into it. The flames turned lavender and blue from the salt in the wood. If the soldiers saw the fire, so be it. I couldn't stay cold and wet. I squatted there, naked, my cock flopped like a shriveled slug on my bluish sack. I savored the warmth while holding my pants in one hand and my shirt in the other to dry them, trying to not breathe in the driftwood smoke. We had learned back in Maine that it could make a person sick.

When I was able to dress again and the fire had caught no one's attention, I picked my way through the big rocks, gathering winkles. We had done this back in Nova Scotia

the two days we waited for the boat. The tiny brown shells
held snaillike creatures that looked a lot like black snot,
but they didn't taste as bad as they looked or felt on my
tongue. They tasted like the ocean, sweet and salty at the
same time. I just wanted food in my belly. It took a long
time to get any substantial meat out of the tiny shells and I
must have sucked on two dozen of them before my mouth
tired. I still didn't have any water and the salt had made my
thirst even more intense, but that would have to wait. Night
had come again, and my head was pounding so badly that I
could see little sparks of light in my peripheral vision. I still
couldn't find it in myself to move far.

I slept like the dead, like a rock falling fast into the
blackness of the ocean.

In the morning I awoke from the pain of my parched
lips. My first thought was that I had to find fresh water.
I couldn't stay on this beach any longer or I would die of
thirst. Almost always there is something in us that wants
to live. It might be precious to say that my desire to survive
was fueled by some deep love for the world, but the truth
is that I got up because I would not allow them to win.
"Them" being everybody who had led to this moment for
me and my family. All of the people who had power when
so many didn't. I wouldn't let them beat me.

So I started walking.

I DON'T KNOW how I had the energy to make my way through those woods and along those lanes. I must have staggered along, intent on finding fresh water yet somehow managing to take in what I saw around me.

Ireland was a more treeless place than I had imagined but it was a glowing green, just as I had heard my parents describe it for the past couple of years. They had had two reasons to aim for Ireland: it was the last place with good water that was still known to take in refugees, and according to my parents, the most powerful of places was supposed to be there: Glendalough. A thin place. Obviously, during those weeks when we were crossing the Atlantic, Ireland had stopped offering sanctuary to American refugees, and now that I had walked miles without one sign of a creek or river, I began to doubt if the water was as plentiful as we had been told. But I had to find Glendalough, for my parents, but also because some little glint of hope, no bigger than a grain of sand, still sparked in me.

Not far from the shore there was a highway, and on either side of it stretched acres of open pastures, crisscrossed with crumbling rock walls, and not much more than burned-out houses and the remnants of what must have once been barns or outbuildings. I could see for miles and in all of the landscape there seemed to be no promise of running water.

I had to stay as unseen as I could, but there was not much hope of that. It would have made more sense to move at night, but I couldn't bear another day on that beach waiting for darkness to fall. I had to have water. I held my hand up to the sun to make sure I was going northeast and crawled alongside the low rock walls to avoid snipers if any were left in this abandoned land.

Across the fields I spotted a narrow strip of trees heavy with dark green leaves alongside the road. I made a mad dash across the open field and found cover within them. I weaved my way through the thin woods until they spread out into a forest. And then, as if it had dropped out of the sky just for me, a large lake opened before me. I cupped the water into my mouth by the handfuls, wetting the whole front of my shirt, then bent down to plunge my face right into the lake. I tasted rocks and ferns and every good thing the water had passed on its way to my lips. A memory of that sensation on my tongue is in my mind right now as I write this for you. I have carried it with me and drawn on it in the hard times I've encountered since. This will always be the taste of Ireland for me.

I sat there, trying to steady myself. Just down the bank from me was a waterfall from a wide creek, and the deep-throated song of the water was a kind of music. I had nothing to carry water in, though. I climbed back up the bank and threw up, a stringy vomit that covered the front of my shirt.

I kept walking. I traipsed through sparse woods and wide-open fields, where I crawled or hunkered low along the rock walls. Sometimes, far away, I fancied I could see the shadow of blue mountains. I didn't see a sign of a person or animal except for the smoldering carcasses of what must have been cattle or sheep on a distant hillside. For a time, I walked along a creek, which I drank from as often as I could.

Once the woods became thick, they were full of birdcall, as if the birds, too, had sought deep shelter to keep the soldiers away. Blue-headed and yellow-chested birds sat in the treetops a few yards ahead of me. When I moved near, they each rose, not all at once, but only slightly staggered, and fluttered a few feet on down to alight in the treetops ahead. It seemed as if the birds were following me yet staying a few steps ahead at the same time. The summer sun shone through the leaves with a kind of green light.

Don't give up, I heard my mother whisper. I saw her face, mouth forming the words. Maybe the ghosts of my parents were walking with me. Mostly I hoped so. But other times I was terrified that I might see their spirits. I couldn't have stood that.

I walked until the sky became a gray smudge, so unlike the black of night back home, but I had been eased into this new way of darkness on the voyage over. I was so tired I didn't even consider the dangers of lying down with no protection around me. There were soft pine nettles on the forest floor whose sweet smell was so inviting that I went to sleep immediately after turning on my side and putting my hands beneath my cheek for a thin pillow. When you are that tired you let fear slip away. And part of me didn't care if someone came along and found me.

PERHAPS THE SMELL awoke me first. Or the tickle of whiskers. In my memory the two things happened at the same time, but the scent is what I remember: a reeking musk, the smell of wildness, of dens ripe with damp earth, of furred legs.

At once I knew that I should not move. I knew an animal was hovering over me. Besides the smell and the whiskers, there was a low, quiet hum in the creature's chest. I dared to open my eyes and a skinny fox was sniffing my face. He sensed the tiny motion and froze, staring at me for a long moment as if considering whether he should sink his teeth

into my nose or not. Behind him the sky was just beginning to lighten with very early morning. I knew there was
another fox, too, because it skittered across my ankles and
then came around so that I caught a glimpse of it behind the
closer one. The scrawnier one took a step forward, his nose
shining black and wet. I remained completely still for what
felt like a very long time but must have only been a minute
or so, before the smaller fox finally lunged forward, pressing its cold nose against my cheek just enough for me to let
forth a loud scream and back away. They scampered off,
tearing through the undergrowth without looking back.

Once my heart stopped thumping, I realized that I was
covered with their stink, lower and muskier than a skunk's
spray, but about as nauseating. The smell lodged in my
mouth and sank into my pores. I got up and walked again
until I found a shallow creek and took off my clothes and
scrubbed them with the rocks I could find. I lay back on
a grassy bank and let the light spread over me while my
clothes dried. I knew I was exposed to the wide world, but
I didn't care in that moment. I laid there until my clothes
were dry. On one hand I wanted nothing more than to get
to this place called Glendalough, since it held the promise
of staying still. On the other hand, the only reason to run
was the hope that there might be more safety there than out
in these hills and pastures.

As soon as I stood to pull on my clothes, I saw the man
and girl walking along the stone fence, perhaps a half mile

from me. I sank back down and crawled up the rise a bit on my belly until I could see them across the wide fields. They were more silhouettes than anything else. I couldn't be sure; it looked as if she was tied to him by a dangling rope. He strode forward as if with great energy and she followed, tripping once and falling. He bent toward her and put forth his hand, but his body language suggested that he was berating her and jerking her back to her feet. I wanted nothing more than to see and talk to another person, yet I could see that these were not the people for that, even though I was so desperate. I lay completely still while they moved over the hill and out of my sight. I was almost certain they had not seen me.

〰 〰 〰

FAR IN THE west greenish-gray clouds were congregating as a storm approached. I had been walking most of the day and my legs were starting to go rubbery beneath me, the blisters on my feet going from piercing pain to numbness to an agony I felt with each step. I paused for a minute and wedged off my shoes and socks, revealing that my feet looked as if they had been underwater all day. My toes were pruned and pink. A large and painful blister rested just below my big toe on the sole of my foot. There was no sun to dry the socks and shoes now, so I shoved a damp sock into each of my pockets. I had no other choice except to slide my miserable feet back into the soggy shoes. I started from the pain, and just as I looked up I saw movement in the dense brush up ahead.

My parents had trained me to move through the world with heightened hearing, seeing, smelling, feeling, so I noticed it in plenty of time to take cover. I slid behind a massive smooth-barked tree—a beech, my mother had taught me that—and squatted down in the beech's exposed and tangled roots, putting my face against the cool dirt to steady my breathing. I looked around to find that there was not so much as a rock or stick within reach that could serve as a weapon. It was foolish of me to have not already chosen one along my way.

I had been startled by little animals I couldn't easily identify. Moles or shrews; I saw only flashes of them and couldn't decipher exactly what they were. But this was different.

There was a sensation in the air that convinced me that whatever was out there was hiding. It was watching me. Maybe waiting for me.

I stayed frozen behind the tree for a good twenty minutes before I dared to move so much as to peep around the tree for a look. When I did, I saw nothing, but I heard movement again. Something brushing against low tree limbs, its feet disturbing the dry leaves on the ground.

I stayed still. I could hear everything around me. The sharp creaking of a tree somewhere deep in the woods. A cacophony of bird conversations. The soft grind of two tree limbs against each other in the passing breeze. I could hear the way the wind was busier up in the very tops of the trees. I could smell the menthol of pine trees, the scent of the black dirt clinging to the beech's roots.

Far away I thought I heard thunder, but it might have been bombing. I was surprised that by now I couldn't tell the difference, as I had heard plenty of both in my lifetime. But I didn't hear anything nearby. And I couldn't stay here forever—if there was one thing I knew for sure, it was that I had to keep moving.

I eased out from my hiding place and put one foot forward, then stopped for two or three minutes. Seeing hearing smelling feeling tasting.

Nothing.

Another step.

Another few minutes of concentration.

I stepped forward again, held my breath.

Nothing.

Another step.

And then, I saw something very white, trying to hide in the shiny green leaves of a huge rhododendron.

I squinted and saw that the white something had spots of black and brown, too. I kept looking until, finally, I could make out a paw. And then, just to the left, two brown eyes looking right at me.

A dog. A beagle.

I hadn't seen a dog in *years*, since I was very small. They had been outlawed when I was a child. Too hard to feed during the Hard Times. Everyone had been forced to give them up, to take them away. I didn't want to think about what had happened to all of the dogs. When I was a child my parents had kept them alive for me by way of a book they had found when we made our way up the mountain in Maine. *The Dog Encyclopedia* had photographs of several different breeds, and beagles had always been my favorite. I liked their speckled legs and large brown eyes and the description of their disposition, so much that I had memorized it: *intelligent, determined, merry, gentle.*

I had started to believe that dogs didn't even exist anymore. But there was one, looking right at me. And strangest of all, the beagle was hiding, not barking. Smart enough to hide.

Later, I would think how stupid I had been to not be afraid. I had overheard tales during the Hard Times of wild dogs roaming the countryside in packs, so hungry they tore into people. I should have climbed a tree or run as fast as I could. But I was so glad to see a set of eyes like that— almost human—that I dropped to one knee.

"Here, boy," I whispered. The first words I had said in two days. "C'mon, little buddy."

The dog rested his chin atop his two front paws and was flattened down as low as he could make himself. His eyes looked eager although he inched himself back at the same time, afraid. But I felt like he was reconsidering his fear.

"I won't hurt you, buddy," I said, although I could hear in my own voice that I didn't sound very convincing. I sounded defeated, tired.

This dog wasn't budging. He was hiding. He let loose a couple of very quiet whines and backed up so that the rhododendron covered his face but left his front paws exposed.

Thunder. Definitely thunder. Close enough now that I could easily tell the difference between it and bombing.

I looked up and saw that the leaves of the trees were turning their backsides to the sky, stirring in the kind of wind that only comes before a rainstorm. Green-gray clouds agitated above us.

The next growl of thunder shook the ground beneath me.

I had to get moving, find some kind of cover, and I wasn't about to trust the dog enough to try to drag him out of his hiding place. So I moved on through the woods, wishing for the dog's company, hating to leave him behind.

The first drops of rain fell as I made my way back down to the creek. I hadn't moved far when I felt the dog behind me. I turned and he lowered his head, one leg crooked up. His eyes were set against mine with such intention that I felt he could read my mind.

Ahead I spotted a group of rocks that together formed a little hut. Rhododendrons crowded in around enough to make a hiding space. I ran to it, ducking into the small opening and sitting on the dirt with satisfaction.

I put my hand through the opening and lowered my face so I could see him clearly again. He was still watching me. "Come on, little man," I said.

And then, the dog came forward.

2

BEFORE

SEAMUS'S STORY

EVEN AS A puppy Seamus roamed free on the island. Every day he awoke at his place beside the man's bed and trotted down the hallway, across the kitchen, and out the special little door in the big door.

Once outside, he yawned and stretched in the morning sun, took in a deep breath of the salt air, and eyed the sky. Usually some gulls were frolicking about and he ran out into the field below to chase them, even though he knew he could not jump high enough to snatch them. Oh, but he would like to. Those gulls had a grand old time making fun of him because he couldn't fly like them. They always wheeled away over the sea, laughing.

Then he'd meander down to the fields. He knew a narrow crevice in the stone fence where he was able to squeeze through and then he was able to run the cows around for a bit of fun until one of them got fed up and stopped and faced him down.

At that he'd squeeze back through the slender gap and go down to the beach to see if anything had washed ashore in the night. Very often there were dead fish that made for a nice, long sniffing but lost his interest within a few minutes. Sometimes there were colored bottles that made a nice music if he pushed them around.

A few times there had been shoes that had washed ashore. He liked to grab their laces and sling them around for a while before he left them at the water's edge. There were shoes to chew on at home as well, if he took the notion.

Lobsters.

Starfish.

Octopuses.

Beach balls, usually flattened.

A baby doll with a dress and bonnet.

The best things, however, were the sticks from the water. Even the bigger ones were light and easy to carry. Once he had struggled home with a piece twice as long as him and dropped it on the porch with a *plomp* that made the man laugh and give him a treat.

Seamus usually went back to find the man up and offering him breakfast. He lay down for a time near his man's feet while he took breakfast or read the morning papers. Later they worked in the garden together. Before tea they had a nice nap together and the man allowed him to hop up on the couch and curl up at his feet. Those were the best naps. By the time the night rolled across the water, Seamus was served his bowl of supper while the man ate his at the table. They watched some television together, and when the nighttime was easing in they went out onto the stoop where his man had his cigarette and scratched Seamus's head as they watched the moon drift over the sea.

"'Tis a good life all in all," the man said nearly every night. Only occasionally he remained silent and on those nights his eyes had water in them.

Every single night the man got down onto his knees beside the bed and folded his hands and bowed his head. His lips moved and Seamus knew to be still there beside him until he had said the word "Amen," which always made Seamus's ears go up because he knew he could get some more attention now.

As long as he could remember, Seamus had always lived here with the man. Nobody ever came to see them. The man put on the same clothes every morning. Now he also used his stick to lean on.

The man was very good to him. Once in a while they rode the shiny red ferry over to the mainland. The man had a car over there and Seamus got to ride in the front seat, where he sometimes put his paws on the dashboard when he became particularly excited. He had to sit in the car when his man went into the grocery but he was allowed to go inside the pub. Everyone in there was always happy to see them. They clapped his man on the shoulder and clicked their small glasses together before sliding the whiskey down their throats. In the pub they also all called out to Seamus. They would all heft their beers or glasses into the air and call out a toast to him and after they had brought their beers or glasses back down to the bar someone would shout, "Now give us a poem, Seamus!" and they'd all laugh.

The man sometimes read aloud in the evenings by the yellow light from the lamp. Often before he read a poem he would say, "Now this one is by your namesake, Seamus."

Then there were new men on the island, all dressed the same and walking stiffly, and the man didn't allow Seamus to roam any more. His little door was screwed shut and he was only allowed to go out if his man was with him, and then only in the small bit of grass right behind the house. He missed the beach and the cows. The gulls still came to taunt him while he was doing his outdoor business and he eyed them with malice, raising a ruckus with his barking.

But then the man told him he couldn't bark anymore. And his man began to do something he'd never done before: rolled up a magazine and swatted Seamus on the rump anytime he barked. For weeks, every day, all day, the man trained him not to bark. Sometimes by swatting his rump with the magazine and sometimes by giving him a treat when he didn't bark at things that usually made him do so:

the man rapping his knuckles on the table, saying aloud, "Is someone there?"

Once the man had gotten on his knees with the water on his eyes and took hold of Seamus's nose and said, "Listen to me, boy. If you are to survive, you must not bark."

Seamus didn't know what he meant.

The skies turned a tarnished silver and cold wind blew up from the sea.

The man stood looking out across the water and listened to the radio all the time. The electricity blinked out but he had a radio that he wound up with a skinny handle and listened to with his ear close to the speaker.

Now he was allowed to sleep in the bed with his man at night. They lay curled up together and even when the planes flew over low and loud in the middle of the night Seamus did not bark.

Then he didn't get his bowl of food anymore, but only what the man brought in from the garden and what was in their pantry. They mostly had potatoes but what they had left now were more rotted than not. Every day there was less.

The ferryman came to the house one day. Nobody ever came to the house but even when he was pounding on the door, Seamus did not bark.

At first his man stood in the kitchen with his ear cocked, waiting for the ferryman to leave. But the ferryman was beating so hard on the door Seamus feared the wood might crack. "Finn! Open the door, Finn!" he pleaded. "Finn, please!"

Seamus's man opened the door just enough to put his face in the space there. The ferryman begged. "You've got to get off the island. We'll all starve to death unless we go to the mainland."

"I'll not leave," Seamus's man said. Seamus whined at his ankle so his man leaned down and scratched him between the ears.

"You'll stay here and die with Seamus? Starve him, too?" The ferryman was full of fury now. "Come on, you mental old man!"

"And do what, take him and let them kill him? No. We'll make do right here."

The ferryman shook his head and then tears were on his eyes. "Father, please," he said. His voice caught on the word *Father* as if he might weep. "I'm begging ye."

But the old man would not budge.

And so in the last days they were alone, although planes still flew over.

One day when the man said he was feeling very well they took a walk. They went up to the high cliffs where they could see the mainland. Seamus's man held something up to his eyes and studied what was happening over there.

"No one about," he said, more to himself than to Seamus.

It was a lovely day, though. The winter had moved on and spring was in full fury. The gorse was blooming as yellow as the butter they used to have. The sun was warm on

Seamus's back, and when his man tired out, they lay down for a while in the grass and let the sunlight soak into their skin.

Seamus could smell the salt and the sand, the yellow of the gorse, the sweetness of the grass, the wood that lay half in the water and half out, the scent increasing each time waves touched it. He could smell the musk of the old man's body. Occasionally the man reached over and gave Seamus's head a scratch or ran his hand down the dog's side, patting him. "Oh, Seamus, I'm thankful you're here with me," he said. And then his voice got jagged and small. "You're a good ole boy, you are."

There was nothing but the wind and the sea and the sunshine that day.

All of the houses stood empty. Even the pub down near the pier, which was empty as well.

Seamus didn't mind that he and his man were the only ones on the island. He didn't mind that it felt as if they were the only ones in the world entire. As long as he had his man, he was happy.

As they walked home, his man had to sit down on the fences lining the road and he breathed hard.

After that day they stayed inside all the time.

His man became very thin and pale. His hair stood in wisps of cottony white. He lay in the bed and coughed. He ate the last of the canned food and always gave Seamus exactly half. Beans, mostly. Sometimes marrowfat peas.

Spaghetti with the most delicious meatballs, dense with congealed fat.

Then he'd lean down and say, "My good old man," and scratch Seamus between the ears.

There were no more single cigarettes on the stoop in the evenings. His man even became too weak to read aloud.

When he was still able, his man unlocked the little door within the bigger door and pointed at it. "Do not leave until you have to. Do you understand, Seamus?"

Seamus tilted his head.

"Only when you *have* to. Do you hear me?"

Seamus heard, but he didn't know what this meant.

One morning he awoke and the old man did not. Seamus licked at his face for a time but still his man did not move. He nudged at the man's hand, and then his face, with his wet nose. Yet the man was as still as a piece of driftwood.

Seamus lay atop his man's chest and looked at him for a long time. He whined. The day passed, and at night he slept. Then the next day. He awoke, aching with hunger, but did not want to leave his man, so he lay there through the next night. He watched the shadows of twilight overtake the room, breathing into the corners. The sun awoke him the next day. The island was very quiet. He had to perk up his ears to hear the crash of the waves down at the shore.

Seamus went to the cupboard and nosed open the door with much difficulty but there was nothing but an empty biscuit tin. He nosed it around the room for an hour until the lid popped open and he was assured that it was empty, which his nose had already concluded long ago.

Seamus went to the little door within the bigger door and poked his head out, looked around. All silence. There was not so much as the chattering of a gull, as if the cows and birds had left now, too, like the people on the ferry had done.

He went back and lay down with his man for many hours, and then, by cover of night, he pushed through the little door within the bigger door and trotted out into the great world again.

SEAMUS WATCHED. HE started at every explosion, scurried back over the dune each time fire snipped at the water, each time the very air expanded almost to bursting. Yet he always returned to watch the girl thrashing about in the water. When all the young people had swum at the beach, he had always gone with them, splashing in after each one who waded far enough out to disappear beneath the water. Sometimes they had yelled harshly at him to hush when he barked at the waves. But then they'd laugh and hug him round the neck and say he was a good boy for swimming in after everyone.

He whined a little—although he had been well trained to not make a sound, not one—as he watched her swimming toward the shore. She only brought her face up enough to draw in air, then she sank back down, taking wide strokes with her arms to move her through the underneath as quickly as she could. In the gathering darkness of night, she was the only one who had swum away from the explosions of fire and water. Seamus had seen this all happen before. This time he would act before it was too late.

He bound down the shore and ran out into the water until he was deep enough to go afloat. The iciness of it was exhilarating and caused a thrill to run all through him. The waves came over his small head and pushed him back toward the island but it was not in Seamus's nature to give up, so he kept swimming, straight for her. She was on her back now, floating.

Behind her the last of the boat disappeared without a sound and Seamus knew that was that.

She was still so far away and now shunts of pain were running down his back legs the way they had on the coldest days when the snow fell on the island and he had to scratch at the door so his man would let him in to warm his paws. He kept swimming straight toward her. She went completely still but then she took a great shuddering breath of air.

As he reached her she wrapped her arms around his neck, which caused the both of them to go under although she was very slender. He thought she might sink them both completely but finally she let go and she was tugging at his collar to bring him up to the surface once more. Now she held on more tenderly, taking the largest breaths he had ever witnessed. The two of them treaded water and then he pulled, pulling her back toward the island. She held on to his collar with one hand, kicking at the water with what strength she had left in her legs and one arm.

Then he felt her let go behind him. He turned and she was stumbling up out of the surf, hunched over and throwing up seawater, then lying half in the water and half on the sand, taking great gulps of air, one hand reaching out for him.

The tracer fire started again, kicking up little clicks of sand all around him. One of the bullets hit her and she fell back as if her shoulders had suddenly been nailed to the beach. Seamus started for the dunes and then he realized that this was not the island. He had gotten turned around in the water and now they were on the mainland. In fact, he could see the sturdy back of the island rising out of the ocean before him. He could see the row of white houses on the hill, the puzzle of stone fences. He could see the very house where he and his man had lived.

More bullets, clicking all about him. He spun and ran, diving into the black rocks along the shore. Bits of the rocks exploded and pinged around him as he was fired upon. He could hear the men yelling and running and then they had her. They were dragging her away up the path in the black rocks. Two men pulled her up the rise as her heels dragged the ground. He sat hidden in a pocket of the wet rocks and watched. He knew he had to be completely silent. His man had taught him that a long while back. Now there were only the sounds of the waves and the unzipping hum of the machine-pods that swooped over the water, looking for anyone else who might still be out there.

But there was no one. Once again, Seamus was alone.

LARK'S STORY

〰 〰

I WAS BORN Before. That's how people talked about it. The Before happened when I was still so little that I had very few memories of the way the world had once been:

Lots of people in our house laughing and singing.

Balloons.

A cake with a candle in the middle.

The sweetness of cake, the slickness of the icing on my tongue. The way the icing turned my lips blue.

Being sprayed with a water hose on the summer yard.

A swimming pool and a float that blew up to look like a dinosaur.

Skipping rocks on a lakeshore with my aunts.

My mother coming home from work, her dress shoes *click click click*ing on the hardwood floor to me, where I played with small metal cars as she pulled me to her.

My father singing along to opera while he cooked, twirling a pasta-covered spoon in the air to the music's rhythm.

Lying back in the grass and laughing while my aunts leaned over me, both of them tickling me at the same time. Their wiener dogs on either side of me, licking at my face. My aunts smiled down at me. There was a long period in my life when nobody smiled like that. Only recently has that returned.

But that's about all I have of the Before. Glimpses, brief encounters.

First there were the fires. Australia burned when my parents were young, then again, and worse, when I was a baby. Later, half of Africa burned, along with most of the land surrounding the Mediterranean. In America, first California burned, but then the entire West, when I was a child. Slowly, at first. Then, all at once. Next the flames took the South. Walls of fire that spread for miles, devouring the land and the houses, the towns and the animals. At first we only saw it on screens. Not in person. Once the crops had been destroyed by the fires the famine began. And then: chaos. Hundreds fighting in the streets for food. Hoarding. An army truck was overtaken by hungry people and the soldiers killed twelve of them in the Louisville Massacre. The pictures of children starving in the streets of Washington D.C. Revelations of the wealthy filling their yachts with food and drifting along the coasts as they waited for things to settle. But everything got worse. The world became smaller, yet louder.

A couple times in the middle of the night I was awakened by my parents talking in the kinds of whispers that end up being loud. For a long time they tried to hide what was happening, but still I kept hearing the same words over and over:

War

Food

Hide

Hungry

ONE NIGHT WHEN I was very small—perhaps five years old—I sat at the top of the stairs so I could hear better. I could see their shadows on the wall at the bottom of the stairs, leaning in toward each other as they sat at the kitchen table. My mother's shadow clutched a shadow of a teacup and my father's shadow stood with his hands over his face. I could hear him, crying. "My baby sister," he said. My mother's shadow got up and went to him as a silence fell over the house.

I sat there for a long time before I padded off to bed.

Another night their muffled conversation awoke me as I realized they were fighting. I found them standing at the foot of the steps. They saw me and my father bolted up the stairs to pull me into his arms.

"I'm sorry, little buddy," he cooed, kissing the top of my head as he carried me down the stairs. My mother stood at the window pale-faced, staring out into the darkness. My father had to say her name to break her reverie. Then she leaned in to embrace the two of us. I had never felt so safe before, swaddled there between them.

And then, when I was seven, they sat me down at the kitchen table and explained what was happening. They took turns talking as if they had rehearsed who would say what.

"There's going to be a war," my father said.

"Where?" I asked.

"Right here," my mother took the lead. "The Fundamentalists—"

I nodded. "The Fundies," I interrupted. I'd been hearing about them as long as I could remember.

"They've taken over. And now we have to fight back because they want everyone to be just like them. They want us to follow their rules."

"And they're not good rules," my father added.

"They want to punish us if we don't obey them," my mother said. "So people are fighting them."

"Will we die?" I asked.

"No, no, no, little man," my father said, and massaged my shoulder with his big hand. "We'll always—we're going to keep you safe."

I believed my father. And he kept this promise until the last moment he was alive.

My parents had always known how to grow food. My mother was a professor of horticulture, so she seemed to know everything about plants and how to save seeds. Both of them knew how to preserve what they grew. They'd been taught during a time when others forgot. Even so, we never had enough. They were hungry most of the time to make sure that I never was. Most of their energy went toward making sure nobody raided our garden at night or broke in to take the jars of tomatoes, peppers, and beans they had canned. Many people we knew weren't as self-sufficient and died of malnutrition or hunger. Bodies were left in the streets. Mass graves were dug in the parks. Bodies were taken out in boats and dumped into the ocean.

The government collapsed and before long everything else did, too. The electricity went out, first for days and then for weeks, and then it didn't come back on at all. That changed everything about our lives. We cooked outside. We cut and split wood to heat the house. My parents read to me at night by the light of a little flashlight powered by a crank on its side. I loved to wind up the light, proud that I was enabling them to see the words a little while longer each evening. I loved *Charlotte's Web* best of all.

At first there were stray cats and dogs everywhere, roaming the streets looking for food. Cats mewed and screamed while dogs barked and howled throughout the night. Then, one night I realized I didn't hear them at all, so I asked where they had gone. "They've all been taken away, darling. There's not enough food for them," my mother said. "It was the humane thing to do." I didn't ask for more explanation because I didn't want to know exactly what had happened to them.

I never knew the details of what all my parents did to fight back, but my mother was often gone for several days, leaving my father and me alone to listen to the gunfire in the distance. Other times injured people were brought to my father in the night. He was a doctor, but he no longer went to work. The hurting people were carried into the back room, some of them screaming out in agony as my mother capped her hands over my ears. I didn't tell her that barely helped.

Sometimes the ground shook from the bombings when the battles between the Fundies and the rebels drew near. Dust drifted down from the ceiling and the light fixtures swayed. We ran down the road with our neighbors at these times, to hide in the highway tunnel that had once carried traffic through the mountain. Everyone ran so fast I thought we might all take flight. I thought if we kept running and our arms kept pumping that our feet would lift off the ground, pedaling against the night sky, and then we would be saved. I caught a glance of my father's terrified face looking back, lit by the red of the fires.

One evening I slipped into the kitchen and saw that my mother had to take my father by the arms and shake him because he was so upset, he was losing his breath. I watched as she eased him into a chair at the kitchen table and then she placed both open palms over her face as she turned away from him. When she brought them down and opened her eyes, she found me watching. She didn't try to comfort me, though. "Oh, Jesus," she said, and turned her face to the wall. Then they were both very quiet, as if there was nothing left to say. After a long silence they told me what happened. I was too young to fully understand, but it was a different world now and there was no use keeping the truth from me.

They told me: My father's sister and her wife had been taken away weeks ago. My aunts, who had fallen in love and gotten married long before the Fundies took over. Now my parents had learned we'd never see them again. Because they loved each other. This was the beginning of the Slaughters.

The priests and professors and artists were killed in the Slaughters, too. The Fundies were in control now and they were the only kinds of believers who were allowed to believe and anyone who defied them disappeared like my aunts. The Fundies always had excuses: they weren't taken away or killed because of who they were or what they believed in or who they loved. Instead we were told they had been caught making bombs, or destroying property during protests. We were told they had been convicted of treason, jailed for stealing, for any reason except the real ones.

We all had to do for ourselves, had to help each other. The food shortages led to people turning against one another or even murdering their own neighbors, but our friends stuck together. There were a dozen of us. At first. Four families from the same little town in Western Maryland where there had once lived hundreds.

One morning the fire-watchers came down from Backbone Mountain to say that the fires were creeping closer. The wall of smoke stood only a few days southwest of us.

We walked for three weeks, moving far up into the mountains, to the Bigelow in Maine, which had once been a nature preserve. My parents had hiked near there on the Appalachian Trail when they were honeymooning and said the place would provide for us. There were waterfalls and springs, several ponds, and a wide lake, they said. Lush woods and clean caves.

Best of all, it was safe, far enough from the cities that the Fundies would not even look there for the rebels who were in the dying days of their fight against them. The place felt like a paradise to me as soon as we arrived. The way the light fell through the glowing green leaves. The sound of the rushing water over the rocks. The view from the top that made me feel like I could see the whole country. I was still young enough to think of our entire journey as an adventure, and my parents were careful to hide their hardship and grief so I could cleave to my sense of wonder.

There was a cave large enough for us to build two small, rough cabins near its opening. By then there were only six of us; we were joined by my mother's best friend, Phoebe, her son, Arlo, who was the same age as me, and her daughter, Sera, who was a year older than us both. There were a few other people on the Bigelow Preserve but we all stayed to ourselves for the most part. My father made friends with some of them. But sometimes it felt like we were the only people left in the world. We lived like the olden times. Like the Laura Ingalls Wilder or L. M. Montgomery books that my parents and Phoebe took turns reading to us in the long nights. We hunted squirrels and rabbit, fished for trout, walleye, and catfish in Flagstaff Lake. We ate berries and plants and the barks of trees. We planted a large garden from the seeds my mother had been saving for years. Once a year she ventured down into the valley to trade for others. She knew how to forage for food and medicine, too. Wildcrafting, she called it. She made salve for our insect bites out of jewelweed, yarrow tincture for colds, fern tea for upset stomachs.

"Everything we need is right here," she told me one day when the summer light fell through the leaves and gave a green glow to her face. I had never loved her more than right then.

She also figured out how to grow plants with the limited amount of light the woods offered. It was too dangerous to cut down the trees; the drones would've been able to see us. In wintertime the bare limbs made us visible, and we hunkered down when we moved through the forest, camouflaged in white. Mostly we stayed in the cave-cabin. We went out only to gather water from the spring or to hunt. Ever since I have thought of the wintertime as the Quiet Times.

But all other seasons Arlo, Sera, and I roamed the woods. I recall the warm months the best. We were raised like siblings, and we did everything together. We climbed to the high rocks and went swimming at the biggest waterfall. We lay in the ferns and talked about what life would be like for us when we grew up. We never said "When this is over" because we didn't realize we were living through something that might have an ending. We just thought we were living. The older I got, the more I talked to Arlo and Sera and the less I talked to my parents.

They were wild and free in a way I never had been: they worshipped their mother, but they disobeyed her and pushed their boundaries in every way possible. Sera, especially. If we were told to not jump into a particular swimming hole because it might be too shallow for that, Sera had to test it out not by wading but by climbing up onto the wet rocks and jumping in. If my parents and Phoebe sat the three of us down and drilled into us that we were not to go to a certain section of the forest, then I would stay as far away as possible, Arlo would lurk at the edges of the forbidden place, doing surveillance from the cedars to see what dangers lurked down there, but Sera would venture into those woods to see for herself. Phoebe tried her best to tame Sera but she couldn't. They were always fighting,

yet they were also so devoted to each other that I often felt
Arlo was left out. He never complained about this, though.
He often liked being alone anyway. Several times he took
off by himself and spent the night out in the deepest part
of the woods, telling only me where he was going. I cherished holding the secret but wished that he had asked me
to come along. I wanted to be with him every minute. Arlo
had an occasional craving for solitude in the same way that
Sera had a constant desire for risk. Unlike either of them,
I hated being alone. Being by myself was my biggest fear. I
was not a needy child, and I didn't long for constant attention. I just liked having people nearby. I liked hearing them
talk and laugh, watching them as they worked. I needed the
noise of others, all the time. Simply the presence of another
human being was a comfort to me, even if we never spoke
or acknowledged one another.

I'd loved being with Arlo more than anyone else, for as
long as I could remember. I liked to study him as he studied leaves or put his hand flat against a tree. Sometimes he
placed his ear to their trunks, too, his unusually green eyes
wide with wonder, but if he ever heard anything he never
told me. I never did, but I didn't tell him that. I couldn't
stand the thought of disappointing him.

There was an old cedar that stood atop the rocky flat
summit on the mountain above our place. We all called
it "the cedar," as if it was the only one in the Preserve.
There were others, but this was the largest one. But it was

Arlo's tree more than ours. He loved its scent so much that sometimes he would rub against its trunk so he could carry its smell home with him. Its bark separated into narrow threads that he sometimes peeled off and put into his pockets. He liked to carry a book with him, and he'd lean against it when he was reading. Sometimes he read aloud to me while I studied leaves and rocks or lay back watching clouds and birds, but mostly he was quiet there, concentrating on the words before him, content with his book and his tree. That's the way I like to remember him best.

Sera was thrilling in different ways; she was always in motion—running, jumping, diving, skipping—and unlike her brother, she was always talking. She'd throw back her head and laugh with her mouth open. She talked of her dreams all the time, what her life would be like someday. The house she would live in. Her travels to exotic lands. She would work with the rebels to overthrow the Fundies. She'd be a codebreaker, she figured, or a medic—part of the rebellion in some way that fought violence instead of participating in it. She had a mane of black hair that often blew into her eyes and mouth if she didn't pull it back. I loved it loose, as wild and free as she was.

By the time I was eleven I knew that I loved them in different ways. I didn't just want to talk to Arlo; I wanted to touch him, all the time. I needed to be near him. Sometimes when the three of us stretched out on the high rocks to feel the sun-baked warmth beneath us, and the sky's heat above us, he would use my thigh for a pillow. Sometimes when we walked down a trail he threw his arm around my neck for a moment. He seemed to not think much of this, but a start ran through me anytime our skin met, causing me to have difficulty swallowing. I wanted to kiss him. I knew that this was outlawed now. I knew what had happened to my aunts. But I loved him; that's all there was to it.

Sometimes in the middle of the nights I awoke to hear my parents talking with Phoebe. Now they said things like:

> *Ireland and Iceland are still taking refugees.*
> *People are staying in the camps for over a year.*
> *It's worth a try.*
> *The water at Glendalough.*
> *The ley lines at Glendalough.*
> *A thin place. They say it's safer there.*
> *Boats are leaving from Little Dover.*
> *Ireland.*
> *Border Patrol.*
> *What choice do we have?*

SOMETIMES WE GATHERED on the high rocks to watch the world spread out below us, the mountains fading away until they became sky, the lake below wide in daytime or streaked by the moon at night.

Once it was just the three of us up there. My parents and me. This was during that perfect time between summer and fall, when the nights were clear and warm, when the woods sang and chirped and cheeped. Sometimes there was howling and sharp cries. A cacophony of birds and insects and animals who had migrated there just as we had, seeking refuge.

There was no moon on this night, but there were so many stars that the sky was more gray than bluish black. We could see every star that ever had been. My mother explained how most of the stars we could see were already gone but we could still see their light. I saw three shooting stars in a row, slanting across the top of the sky.

"Before, we could've never seen a sky like this. Because of all the lights," my father said. "Do you understand?"

I nodded. I was twelve years old by this time and I understood everything. Or at least I thought I did. I understood that my father was not just telling me that we were able to see more stars now because of the greater darkness. He was also telling me that there was a positive even in the worst situations. My father was saying we had to latch onto moments like this to keep from giving up.

Not long after that, my parents told me that Sera and I weren't allowed to go off into the woods by ourselves anymore.

"We're not ever alone," I said, thinking this was ridiculous. "Arlo is always with us."

"Sometimes you have been alone, though," my father said. "Listen. From now on you can only be with her if someone else is there, too."

"It's not safe," my mother interrupted before he could say more, clenching her jaw, and then I knew why, but I wanted them to say it aloud.

"What's happened?" I asked, although I thought I knew. "Tell me."

My father took hold of my upper arms and put his face close to mine. "Promise us," he said. "Promise us that you won't go anywhere alone with Sera."

"Why *not*?"

"Because it's not safe, and that's all the explanation you need," my mother said, angry. She didn't like back talk. "Mind us."

"Do you understand, Lark?" my father asked, his dark eyes so close I could see flecks of gold in them. As always he was the gentler of the two.

"If Sera were to have a baby, Lark," my mother said, but then I didn't think I could stand to hear her say any more, so I ripped myself away and ran into the woods, down the paths that I could have navigated in complete darkness, running until I was up on the high rocks and found Sera sitting there, alone. Her mother had had the same talk with her today. She had taken Arlo with her so she could get away, then told him to leave. He was swimming down at the creek even though we were never supposed to swim alone.

We sat looking out across the mountains as clouds striped and unstriped the sun, decorating the endless trees below us with jagged shadows. "They don't want us to be alone," she said.

"They told me."

"They're afraid you'll knock me up," she said, "which is hilarious." She laughed, turning to me. A rectangle of sun fell directly across her eyes. She leaned in quick and put her lips on mine. One soft touch. I hoped that my mother had followed me down the trail and would catch us.

Sera pulled back and drew her forearm across her mouth,

disgust on her face. "God, that was stupid," she said. "I just had to do it because they told us not to."

"It's all right," I said. "I don't mind."

"I know you're in love with my brother."

"Don't say that," I whispered. I had the urge to cap my hand over her mouth, but I didn't, knowing she would throttle me. "Don't ever say that out loud."

"Not like there's anyone around to hear us, Lark. Nobody's going to come and take you away here."

I went silent. I had known who I was for some time now, of course, but Sera speaking it out loud made it more real. I looked down at my hands and was aware of my breathing, which felt like small blocks of air that came from far down in my lungs before being exhaled.

Sera scooted closer to me and laid her head on my shoulder, leaning against me. "It's all right," she said, whispering now. Not because there was anyone to hear, but only because she hesitated to break apart the quiet I had fallen into. "Nobody knows except for me, and I'm not saying a word."

"He doesn't?"

"Not yet," she said. "But he will."

"How obvious is it?"

"Not so much. I'm just incredibly perceptive," she joked. "So, if you two fall in love and become a couple, you'll have each other but you will have to take care of me when I'm a dried-up old virgin stuck on this mountain in my eighties.

Never been kissed except one pitiful time by my brother's lover. Jesus, I knew our futures were bleak, but this is ridiculous."

I put my arm across her back, and she snuggled in closer. We sat there watching the sky change without speaking but she couldn't stand the quiet. She stood and put her hand out to pull me up. "Time to go. Let's walk back together and tell them we had sex, just to fuck with 'em."

THREE MORE YEARS passed like that, me pining for Arlo. For his part he treated me like his best friend. Like an extension of himself. The three of us had been raised there with no one else except our parents, so the connections ran deep and wide. We might have been raised like siblings, yet we weren't. The longer we were all up there together—just the six of us—the more Sera and Arlo and I needed something of our own, something that no one else knew about. My parents had each other. Phoebe's whole world revolved around Sera and Arlo. But as teenagers Arlo and Sera and I felt we only had each other. Everybody has to have something to call their own. So I didn't tell him how I felt. Too afraid he would be repulsed and too frightened that it would change our trio. Sometimes Sera encouraged me to tell him. "Just lean in sometime and give him a kiss," she told me, watching me stare at him as he stacked wood. Her words might have been encouraging but the way she said them lacked the zeal that usually accentuated everything she said. I had been told my whole life that two boys or two girls who loved each other could not exist in our world. That time had come and gone, a brief, unimaginable time when there was often derision toward people like my aunts loving one another, but not laws forbidding it.

I worried that Sera might have similar feelings for me. Other times I thought about how she might never have anyone of her own. I never wanted to leave that mountain, but I knew that she did, and I knew that if we didn't, she'd always be alone.

Those were holy years, our time in the Preserve. I knew that, even then. Soon Arlo and I would be sixteen, the age that boys had to join the Fundamentalist forces or be declared as traitors who would be sent to a work camp, or worse. At sixteen Arlo and I would be of age to join the Fundamentalist forces or be declared as traitors who would be sent to a work camp, or worse. If the Fundies found our family, my father would be forced to swear his allegiance to their cause. He would have stood against a wall to be shot before he would have done that. My mother, Phoebe, and Sera were also living forbidden lives since they were not dressing or behaving the way the Fundamental Laws demanded of women. The new laws had declared them as inferior, as little more than the property of my father. And if they knew how I felt, I would be put on the same trucks or trains that had carried my aunts away.

For the most part I tried to not think about these things, but this knowledge was always at the edge of my consciousness. Yet Sera, Arlo, and I were content. We had our own world of waterfalls and warm rocks. A world that revolved around the cedar tree, where we often sat with our backs to the trunk, having intense conversations as the tree's musk seeped into our skin until Arlo tired of human company and took off for the cloak of the woods.

This is not to say things were perfect, but in retrospect I can see that they nearly were. Sometimes my parents argued and wouldn't speak for a couple days. Sometimes I argued with them and we all three sank into our moods. Very often Sera and Phoebe fought. Rarely did Arlo or Sera and I argue, although there were times when I felt so angry at Arlo for superficial or illogical reasons because I couldn't tell him how I really felt about him. When Arlo was upset, he didn't speak it but merely went away for a day or two. Sometimes my mother and Phoebe argued, but they always made up before long, crying and holding on to one another like they both understood the other's grief in a special way. They had grown up together, long before they were neighbors, and they had a way of communicating with each other with just a look.

For the most part, we were happy. We all worked together. We helped each other survive. I gathered ramps, fiddleheads, and chokeberries with my mother in the forest. I cleaned the squirrels when Phoebe brought them back from her hunts. Dressing them was messy, greasy work. I hated skinning them to reveal their taut pink muscles. I hated the necessity to cut off their paws for the coat to come free more easily. I preferred cleaning the fish that Sera brought

back from the ponds and streams. There was something less
violent in the way the sharp knife slid between the scales
and meat, then clicked across the tiny ribs to free two perfect filets. I helped my parents in the garden with the beets,
carrots, cabbages, potatoes, kale, turnips, parsnips. Arlo
cut and stacked wood or built things we needed: a trellis
for cucumber vines, a smokehouse for curing deer meat,
a fence to keep the animals out of the garden. We worked
all the time, but my parents and Phoebe made sure that
they made fun times for us, too. Usually we did everything
together. "Strength in numbers." My mother said this a lot.

On the first warm day of the year when I was sixteen,
we went to our favorite waterfall for a swim. The falls burst
out of the mountain in a torrent, spreading in a willow
shape over a bulbous gray rock that made a wide shower fall
right over a wide pool. There were rocks beneath, where we
could stand and let the water massage our backs, but parts
of the pool were deep enough to dive into as well.

We whooped and hollered. We stood for a long time
under the falls, letting its water flow over our heads and
bodies. We dove and swam and floated. My mother and
Phoebe lay back on the mossy rocks, relaxing. My father
splashed with Sera, Arlo, and me. He dove and swam while
we did. We were about as happy as people could possibly
be back then.

Always, I watched Arlo. One spring day I could see how
much his body had changed during the past few winter

months when we had not seen each other stripped down. In warm weather he and I and my father always went to bathe together but during the winter we all did this privately with a dishpan of heated water and a washrag. He was a man now. Although we were the same age I felt scrawny in comparison. Despite working all the time, I had hardly any muscles. He did, though. He also had a shimmering trail of brown hair that ran from his navel down into the waistband of his shorts, as well as a shadowy patch on his chest. There were two dimples at the bottom of his back that always drew my eyes to them. There was something graceful about the careful way he moved now. I tried to not look at the way his shorts clung tightly to him when he climbed up the slippery rocks to jump into the swimming hole again.

Sera missed nothing, though. Sera and I were at the front as we hiked through the woods, with my father in the back, always watching for interlopers. Today Arlo walked with him. He worshipped my father, and they had an ease between the two of them that I envied. The light fell through the glowing green leaves and the smell of spring carried through the forest. "Fecund," my mother had called this scent one day. Wild and lush.

I watched Sera as she strolled in front of me, holding her hand up to brush against low-hanging leaves. She was always touching everything. Her hair, which she usually wore pinned up, was spread across her shoulders and down her back, still damp from our swim.

All at once, Sera took off running, and looked back at me to let me know I was supposed to chase her. My father hollered for us to wait, but when we ran on he let it go. My mother and Phoebe didn't, though. I could hear them calling angrily after us. They were always so afraid that we might eventually crash into each other and produce another mouth to feed that it would have been kinder of me to have told them the truth and quelled their fears. I wasn't courageous enough to do that yet. They all must have stayed exhausted from keeping us apart, terrified of what might happen when we were alone.

Sera could always leave me in the dust when she ran. She leaped from the path and went into the richest part of the forest, where we were not supposed to go and where ferns and laurel grew large and exotic. I could tell by the way she was moving that she had been here before, but I had not. Her secret place. I had one, too. When you live with only five other people on top of a mountain for years, you find ways to make a life of your own any way you can. In the times when Arlo went away on his hermitages, I often went to my own place, too, wishing he was there with me. I ran after Sera until we came to a wide creek crashing down out of the mountain, flanked by piles of moss-covered boulders on either side. She scrambled over the big rocks and expertly shimmied across the creek to stand on its far shore, bending to pant for breath after her hard run, then standing with her hands on her hips as she took deep breaths and kept her eyes on me with a strange little smile on her face.

"You have to tell him, Lark," she said.

"But what if he isn't like me?"

"He is. I know my brother."

"What are the chances of that, though. Of—"

"I think we're all a little bit that way. That's why it scares people so much. But some of us are all the way in one direction or another. Like a spectrum. I read an article about it in one of Mom's magazines." Phoebe had found five magazines in a burned-out library during our journey, miraculously immaculate in a room that had managed to escape the worst of the blaze. Their pages were curled and stiff, but she treasured them as much as the six books we had kept through all of this. "I'm not completely sure where Arlo falls on there, but it's closer to your side than mine. I know that."

"How?"

"I know every one of you inside out. Analyzing you five has been my life's work," she said. "What the hell else do I have to do?"

Then she leaped from one rock to the other on her tiptoes, as light as a moth, over the mossy stones tumbling down the creek. She stopped beside me, so close our shoulders touched. "Do you know what I'd give to have a chance like that, to love somebody? Don't waste it." She left then, headed back down the trail toward home before the search party came for us.

That night, after supper, we sat around the fire with our parents. Phoebe played her fiddle and sang. My mother would never sing alone but sometimes she and Phoebe harmonized together. Always John Prine songs, which they both loved. *You've got gold in you*, they'd sing, or *Make me an angel that flies from Montgomery*.

The older I got, the more melancholy settled in me on nights like these, as if I could feel the approach of whatever force would destroy our lives there first: the fires or the Fundies. These were my teenage years, when I had so many questions about why our country was crumbling, why the Fundies got to make decisions about our lives when we didn't even know them, why anyone would be repulsed by me loving Arlo. Most everyone I had ever known was dead, so I thought a lot about my own mortality. I wondered if death was being alone in some void, the thing I feared most. I am an old man now and still wonder these things. The difference now is that I am content to let the mystery be. But in those days the fire of wondering nearly consumed me.

Sera sat on one side of me, and Arlo on the other. He stretched his arms out wide above him to accentuate a yawn. When he brought his arms down, his left elbow slid along my forearm. Enough to send my body into a frenzy. Like every time, that little bit of contact sent a start all through me, like a cold chill, only in a good way. But Arlo seemed unaware of his power and kept his gaze on his mother's fiddle. I looked away from him to see that my

father was staring at me. I could tell that he knew everything about me.

NOT LONG AFTER that night, Arlo and I were sent to hunt
morels. My father had sighted a large patch of them on a
shady hillside right where the thickest part of the woods
touched the edge of the wide wildflower pasture that led
down to the lake. We had found several growing along the
length of two rotting elm trees that had fallen together in
the past couple of years and our baskets were full in no
time. On the way back we passed right by our best swimming hole and the June heat begged for us to get in. Arlo
peeled off his shirt, then his pants, standing naked with
his back to me. And then he turned. He was perfect to me,
but I glanced away, embarrassed, and when I did, he ran
and jumped into the lake, pulling his knees up to his chest
in a cannonball that resulted in a splash that reached for
the sky.

I took off my clothes and jumped in, too, hitting the cold
water, sinking down to the rocky bottom of the ancient
swimming hole. My feet came to rest against the chill there
and I sat still for a minute with my arms spread wide, listening to that eternity-like sound of being underwater. All
stillness. The wildest of places.

I pushed myself up and burst to the surface. When
I opened my eyes, Arlo was in front of me. Still he said
nothing, but then his slick arms were around me, one hand

clutching the back of my shoulder, the other grasping my hip, and our mouths met so hard that I heard our teeth click.

He tasted and smelled like the mossy rocks and the clean water, like mountains made only of cedar. I can still draw that scent up to me, all these years later. On occasion when I am caught up in all of my remembering, that smell floats to me. Maybe it's only cedars nearby I'm smelling. Maybe it's him, come to visit.

There was movement in the large shining leaves of the giant rhododendrons that leaned toward the creek from the high banks, and we both pulled back from each other at the sound of feet running away on the soft path. Sera, I thought, and he must have as well. Arlo swam away from me as if nothing had happened. He did a couple of flips underwater, then climbed out and put his clothes on with his back to me, silent.

I stood in the middle of the pool with my hands floating on either side of me. "Arlo," I said.

"We can't," he said, and sat down on a rock to put on his shoes. I knew he was right. There was too much to risk, too much to lose.

MY MOTHER LOOKED away when I came into our house, so I knew she had been the one on the trail. She didn't say anything until that evening when I left the fire, saying I wanted to go to bed early. She followed me in, the scent of woodsmoke strong on her clothes in the closeness of the cabin as she stood near. I turned to face her.

"It's all right," she said, at last, and drew me into her arms. She was not a blatantly affectionate person but on this night she held me tightly. "But promise me you'll never let anyone else know if we leave this mountain," she said with her mouth very close to my ear. "No one can know but the six of us. It's too dangerous."

I promised.

From then on Arlo and I were a couple, just like that, and no one treated us any differently than they had before. We were only seventeen, but we knew that life was short for most of us in those days. We were adults in the eyes of our parents. Phoebe was more terrified that Fundies might find out about us some day, but here on the mountain we were safe. My father helped us build our own little cabin near the other two. One room, a small fireplace, a dirt floor. But it was mine and Arlo's. Often Sera stayed with us, too, and we'd sit up late laughing and playing rummy with our ragged deck of cards. On those nights Phoebe was the only one of us who was alone. Nobody seemed to worry about this except for me; since I had such a fear of solitude, I was always conscious of those who were left by themselves. I never said as much to Phoebe, however, and sometimes I could tell by the way she looked at me that she thought I was the reason so much of her time was spent on her own during those days.

I loved having Sera with us, but I have to admit that the best times were when it was just me and Arlo. For two years we were as free as two people can be.

To taste and be tasted. Every part of us humming and alive. If you are very lucky it happens occasionally that your body fits with someone else's in such a way that you feel you are not two separate people but one being, that you've gone beyond the physical. To know each other by heart. To sit and be silent with someone else. To feel as if you are alone, yet with someone. To feel safe.

Two entire years of contentment. And then, everything changed.

THE FIRES CAME to us.

We watched them, getting closer for a week, easing up on either side of the lake. Once the fire jumped the river, we knew we would have to leave. A sadness like that latches itself around your neck. We all carried it with us as we chose what to take with us, as we said goodbye to the place that had protected us so well. Arlo ran his hands down the trunk of the cedar tree and then held his scented fingers to my and Sera's faces. If we had to carry the grief we might as well take some of the beauty with it. There was always room for that.

We left it all to burn. The cedar. All of the cedars, all of the trees. The nests of whip-poor-wills and owls. The cabin. Sometimes I still lie awake at night, imagining what happened to all of the things we had loved. The blackened walls of our cave. The charred remains of those trees we had known so well. I guess the only things that remain are the rocks and the water. The river, the creeks, the falls, singing along in a barren landscape. The water doesn't know.

At the river we were joined by a dozen strapping deer, their ears flicking toward the fire as they wondered what would happen next. Normally we would've killed the deer for food, but nobody moved. On down the river we saw a black bear loping, families of possums and raccoons and groundhogs swimming furiously, not as trusting as the deer.

Then, we walked.

SIX HUNDRED MILES, from the Bigelow Preserve in Maine to Little Dover, Nova Scotia. Eighteen days, twelve hours a day. We met many good people who helped us along the way. A barn offered for shelter, a meal shared, kind words. We evaded the Fundamentalist soldiers who patrolled the little towns to make sure everyone was complying with the laws. There were robbers along the way that we managed to avoid, beggars who made it difficult to refuse them with their fearful desperation and their hungry children, the shame of begging heavy on their shoulders. We gave them what we could. I still remember their faces.

While in the valley to trade seeds, my mother had learned about the boats. We had no money, but the seeds were light enough to carry and she had hoarded them, saving for when she'd have to trade them for our survival. Seeds had become among the most valuable things in the world, and my mother kept them strapped to her body at all times, even in her sleep. The seeds would be especially valuable when we tried to barter for passage across the ocean. My father being a physician would help, too. Phoebe had been a teacher, but that didn't matter to people much by then. But she was also strong. She was slender and small, but her arms and legs were well muscled. Her hands were firm and her fingers were calloused. She wasn't afraid of anything. Sera, Arlo, and I were used to hard work and could offer only that. We figured a boat making the crossing would need people like us, even if we couldn't pay.

We kept to the woods as much as we could, heading toward the Canadian border, where we knew there would be patrols by the Canadian soldiers to keep us out of their country, and by the Fundies, who would try to force us to stay. The trees glowed green with springtime and the leaves were no bigger than squirrel ears. At night we all slept together atop the huge down comforter we took turns carrying on our backs, like an enormous white mushroom attached to our bodies. In warm weather it was good to lie upon, and in the cold it offered warmth.

We crossed the border at the St. Croix River, which we knew would be the hardest part to patrol. We each built our own small rafts that were just large enough for us to lie down upon so that we could hang our arms and legs over the side and swim safely with the bound limbs of the raft keeping us afloat. Our most valuable items were strapped to our backs above the waterline. Thankfully there was a steady downpour the night we arrived to cross, so there was not so much as starlight to reveal us as we eased through the black water. The crossing was no more than a half mile, but we moved so carefully that we spent two hours slipping across the cold river, expecting gunshots from the border patrol to pock the water around us at any moment. But we reached the Canadian shore to find the woods singing with the earliest insects of spring. I could hardly believe that we had made it with no obstructions.

We walked on for a couple more hours by cover of night, cold and miserable in our wet clothes, before the sky started to fade into blue along the eastern horizon. My teeth chattered and my legs chafed with every step. We hoped for a cave where we might build a fire to dry ourselves and gain relief from the pounding rain but had no luck. The land here was much flatter than we were used to. The woods were mostly free of brambles, and we were able to move through with little to impede us except for the rain, which fell harder and colder now. When daylight came, we would be far enough from the border to not be so cautious, but we would still hide in the woods until the cover of darkness came again so we could move safely on with eight more days of walking ahead.

Phoebe, leading the way, made the call of a mourning dove, which we all knew as a signal to stop and listen. I stopped so suddenly that Arlo stepped on my heels. He took hold of my hand and held it while we waited. Phoebe had heard something but was too cautious to speak so that we might know why we were waiting. We stood like that for a a long while, waiting for something to happen, for there to be another sound. As we did the sky lightened and a dusk-like haze hovered around us.

As soon as Phoebe motioned us on, shots rang out. Arlo pushed me to the ground and spread himself over me. I couldn't see anything else except for the soles of Sera's shoes just in front of my face. I put my arm out and took hold of one of her ankles to comfort her. Then we could hear the trunks of the trees being struck by bullets. *Snip snip snip.* Then, no more, as if someone had taken the sniper out in our defense. I thought I heard the footsteps of people hurrying away. The ringing in my ears was increasing. We lay still for what seemed a long while but was actually a handful of minutes, waiting. Not speaking. Trying to not even breathe. Listening. We could hear only remnants of the recent rain, dripping onto the leaves.

At long last my father sprang to a crouching crawl, scrambling through the leaves to draw attention and see if anybody was still about. When there were no more shots, he went to standing very still for a time as he looked through the springtime woods, tempting the sniper to show himself.

"Okay, I think it's clear," he said finally, and then Arlo stood, and that's when he saw his sister lying on the ground before us. A pool of blood on her back revealed the gunshot that had gone through her body. She was gone. Arlo fell to his knees beside her and cried out. "Please, not her," he howled, pulling Sera onto his lap.

Then I saw the wound in his side; blood was burbling out like milk from a jug. Phoebe pressed her palm over the wound, but the blood seeped out anyway. "Lark—" Arlo said, his eyes widening.

My father went to work on him right away. He took out his medical kit, an apron that he unfolded to reveal his instruments, as well as vials and little tins of dried herbs and roots. He spread the apron out on the ground beside him and moved with careful precision. As he cleaned the wound, I offered my hands for Arlo to squeeze while he bit down on a piece of cloth. The blood continued to flow from his side. The look on my father's face told us all there was nothing he could do.

"I'm sorry," Arlo said, his voice hoarse and low. Phoebe leaned over Sera now and was whispering frantically to her, but all I could focus on was Arlo's face going ashen. He stared at me, not saying anything. I bent and put my mouth on his until he was gone.

Phoebe pushed me aside, running her hands down his face. She kissed his forehead and his eyes and his mouth. She had fallen directly between her two children and pulled each of them onto her hips as she sat in the dirt. My mother had come to me and held me from behind.

"It's all right, my darling," Phoebe said to Arlo. "It's nothing. Nothing at all." The pain in her voice was almost too much for me to bear. "Oh, my little darling, my little bird," Phoebe whispered, as she kissed the tops of Sera's hands.

After a time I realized that the morning was brightening. A breeze moved through and the big cedars nearby sounded like a river moving.

Sometimes, even now, I am aware of Arlo walking alongside me. He is like a breath of air that appears beside me sometimes when I am crossing a wide field on my own. Or when I am standing up on the mountain, watching day slide over the world. I never acknowledge this presence, but I know he is with me all the time.

I watched the wind in the low limbs of the cedars, and I disappeared into them. A calmness had come over me by then that I now recognize as a kind of numbness.

I was not in my right mind.

All at once I was aware of Phoebe striking my mother across the face with the back of her hand, as if I heard the sound before I saw it happen. The wide force of her entire forearm swinging through the air and knocking my mother down. I rushed forward, only wanting to get to Arlo one more time. That's all that I cared about. But Phoebe was not letting anyone go near her children. She was a wild animal. In one slick motion she had drawn her hunting knife from its sheath on her hip and held it low before her.

"Don't come near us," she told me, "or I'll cut you wide open. This is *your* fault. You took both of them from me a long time ago." Her face was a snarl of hatred. "God damn you to hell for this."

My mother said Phoebe's name, a hand to her swelling face. Phoebe jutted the knife in her direction and told her to shut her mouth. They loved each other like sisters; I knew that much. They had certainly been through more together than most sisters. But that Phoebe had died with Sera and Arlo. I could see in her face that she was gone, the woman who had survived with us. The woman who had played the fiddle in the evenings and sung in her own sad way.

Arlo lay with his palms up as if receiving the morning. The new light dappled leaf shapes on Sera's face. Gone, gone.

My father rushed and grabbed Phoebe from behind, clamping his arms around her torso, but she was too quick for him. She brought the knife down into the top of his right thigh and gave the handle a twist before drawing it back out and pulling it high into the sky, gaining momentum to plunge it into his back. But my mother caught her before she could, lunging at her so hard that both of them hit the ground and the knife slipped from her grasp. Phoebe scrambled to grab hold of it and crawled in the leaves and dirt until she had reached Sera and Arlo again. She sat between them, holding the knife out toward us in her trembling hand.

"Leave us alone," she said, her mouth barely moving, her eyes glazed.

The three of us had eased away from her to the other side of the cedar copse. My mother examined my father's leg. "We have to keep moving," she said. "We're still at least eight days' walk from the boats, and he won't be able to walk on his own." She was in matter-of-fact mode, which is what happened when she felt she was in total chaos. "We'll have to help him. We'll have to build a cot and carry him."

"We can't leave her out here like this," my father whispered.

"What other choice do we have?" my mother said. "She's out of her mind. She'll kill us."

"Give her some time," my father said.

"No," my mother said. "She's gone."

I couldn't stand the thought of leaving her here with their bodies. "We can't leave without burying them. We have to."

"They're gone, Lark," my mother said. "It doesn't matter."

Nothing matters, I thought.

"Be easy with him," my father told her.

"They're dead and all we can do is keep going," she said. "We don't give up, and that's all there is to it."

I couldn't listen any longer. I moved away from them, back through the cedars toward Phoebe. I would fight her if I had to. She could kill me if she had to, but I was going to see Arlo one more time. I was going to kiss him goodbye.

But Phoebe was already fading away, one arm thrown around Arlo and the other fastened around Sera. She had cut her own wrists and the blood covered them all. I bent and held her head in my arms and she kept her eyes on me until she died.

My mother and I buried them quickly in shallow graves while my father tried to rest on a mossy bank. I used all of my fury to dig the wide grave. We dug down as far as we could with rocks and limbs and then we stacked the rocks atop them. I sank to my knees and my grief started quiet and then grew to a wail from some animal part of me, a wail that exhausted me but did not last very long. I lay with my face against the ground for a time while my mother sat beside me, her unmoving hand a presence on the back of my neck. I bit into the ground and tasted the dirt. I choked down a swallow of it, then sat up and steadied myself.

I asked my mother if she could say some kind of prayer for them and she scoffed. "For what? There is nothing," she said. "This is all there is."

I didn't reply, but I did close my eyes. I didn't know what there was to believe in, but I had always felt there was something, humming in the air around us, even if I couldn't name it. I must have asked this force to let them rest. I had nothing poetic in me at that point. But it felt wrong to leave them out there without a word, without believing in something. Now that I am an old man, I know that there is much to believe in, although I do not have a single word for it the way some people do. To be too certain about belief is a dangerous thing.

THE CLOSER WE got to Little Dover, the more we had to dodge the roving troops of soldiers who were supposed to prevent Americans from crossing the border over to Canada. There was nothing much left here. Pine trees and seashore. Our feet were bleeding and raw by this time. So were my hands, from holding on to the pine branches we had fastened together to carry my father; Phoebe's plunging of the knife had caused serious damage and, now, infection in his leg. Thick branches were too heavy, so we had had to string together several smaller limbs that not only had some give to them but also made for a lighter load. My mother and I were both strong but carrying him nearly killed us. I don't know how we did it. But you can do a lot of things when you have no other choice.

All at once the harbor knitted itself into being and there was the large rubber raft that would carry us out to the boat. Several men stood in the blackish water struggling to anchor it. Men with iron rods or barbed bats hurried us along. We knew they wouldn't take my father if they saw how badly injured he was, so he swallowed his pain and leaned on me enough to walk down the bank to the raft. That's how determined a man he was. His pants were so filthy the bloodstains barely showed. Meanwhile, a horrible pus had overtaken the wound on his leg, which had seemed to open wider instead of healing in the eight days it had taken us to get here.

By this time we were such ghosts that it's a wonder any of us could feel anything at all. Sometimes I thought we were already dead without knowing it.

My mother was negotiating with a sharp-faced woman who had made it known she was in charge here. "We'll work around the clock," she said. The woman listened with no expression on her face, but she had a habit of moving her long nose about like a rabbit sniffing at the air. Then, my mother lied: "I've been sailing all of my life, and I taught him."

"You and the boy can go on, but not him," the woman said, nodding her pointy chin to my father. She had not been fooled by his attempt to seem fine. Then my mother shoved a packet of seeds into her hands without a word. The woman ripped the small brown envelope open and poured them out onto her palm, moving them around with one dirty finger.

"Go on," she said, returning the seeds to the packet and shoving it into the folds of her blouse.

We climbed on. The bottom of the raft was so thin I could feel each movement of water beneath us. Occasionally the great waves washed over the sides, and I was instructed to take up a bucket and bail out the water. A salty swell struck me in the mouth and caused me to choke on the sea-water, and then I realized that I was still alive.

The raft motored through the raging sea, battling the wild waves. Up ahead the boat bucked on the ocean. Behind it the sky was dimming into night. From a distance we could see that the deck was crowded with people, and even over the sound of the crashing waves and the raft's small motor I could hear the din of all the humanity aboard. I could see other rafts in the water now, all heading toward the boat, too. There was no way we would all fit.

People clambered up on all sides of the boat and the passengers already up there were yelling, trying to stop the crew from allowing more to board. The boat rocked with the beseeching weight on either side of it. I had to ignore all of the chaos and focus on climbing up the rope ladder with my father holding tight to my back. As soon as I started up, I knew that I could not do it. My mother climbed up and bartered with the men, and then four of them extended their large hands and pulled me up, my father strapped to my back as if he were my child. I fell to the wet deck of the boat, my lungs aching from the salty air I had drawn in so deeply.

Almost immediately the anchor was pulled up and the boat lurched over a huge wave, and the long journey across the black ocean lay ahead of us. We left behind people who'd fallen off trying to board, others on the rafts, watching with blank expressions, knowing they had been left to die there. I could hear them. The misery of them. The anguish. I could hear a baby crying out there, a woman wailing, an old man begging us to not leave him. I hear them sometimes, still, in my nightmares.

I watched North America until I could see no more of it. First just a thin purple line on the horizon, then a black silhouette, then: nothing. *Goodbye forever*, I thought, but did not say aloud.

3

SEAMUS AND LARK

Because their love of Earth is deep,
And they are warriors in accord.

—GEORGE MEREDITH,
"THE LARK ASCENDING"

I WAITED. I was so tired I could barely move, but somehow, I thought if the dog might come near and put his wet nose into the palm of my hand, I would be reenergized. This one act would be enough to get me through. And so this was the first time he saved me.

The dog had come forward but now he hesitated, took one step back, his brown eyes locked on to my face, trying to read any sign that might be found there.

"It's okay, buddy," I said, and I realized that even my lips were tired, even the muscles in my face. I felt slack-jawed, like weights had been attached to my pants legs and the hem of my shirt. The rain was falling quiet and soft like small feet stamping the leaves, but I knew that any minute the sky would open up; the sound of thunder was shifting closer and louder. "Please," I said to the dog. I did not want to be alone.

He ventured close enough for me to pet him. There were small twigs and cockleburs caught in his fur, but his coat was somehow clean and smooth, as if he had been careful to bathe and groom himself on his journey. I leaned down and he startled me with a lick to the nose. He was wearing a red collar, bright against his black-and-white coat. I took hold of it and there was a small round silver medallion hanging from it that read *SEAMUS, Sherkin Road, F91.*

I whispered the dog's name, only knowing how to pronounce it "Shame-us" because my father had loved Seamus Heaney so much. I caught sight of him back on the mountain in Maine, standing before the high flames of our fire, one hand floating out in front of him like a bird, the other ahold of his belt buckle as he called out, "Death would be like a night spent in the wood." At the end of the poem, he'd put his hands together and looked briefly skyward to give credit: "Seamus Heaney, ladies and gentlemen," he'd say. Then he'd bow as we all clapped.

I took the dog's ears in each hand and felt them in my palms, smoothed down his neck and along his back. He was looking at me as if he had been craving such a massage for a long while. Seamus's eyes had sorrow in them—this old boy knew what deep loss was, just as I did. Two creatures can always tell that about one another.

The rain on the leaves above our heads increased its

chatter, so I knew we had to make a run for the rock shelter. I went for it, hoping he would follow, and he did, galloping behind with his front paws high in the air and his haunted eyes right on mine. We made it just before the downpour unleashed, a great cracking of the sky that sent a sudden torrent of rain along with lightning and groaning thunder.

Inside the rock shelter, I could see that it was no natural occurrence—someone had built this, ages ago. Two huge, flat rocks stood on their edges with another big flat rock atop it for a roof, all leaning against an ancient tree on either side and a rockface at the back that had kept it from tumbling over for centuries. The spot was dry but small, and the dog had no other choice but to curl up near me to avoid the rain splashing in. We were well hidden from anyone who might pass by, yet we could see out past the rhododendron leaves and hear anyone approaching. And there were plenty of jagged rocks lying about that would fit easily enough into my hand for weapons. If anyone came near I could fight them with a pointed stone fitted just between two fingers to get in at least one good lick. All in all, this was the safest I had been in the three days since the boat had sunk.

Seamus had the sweet, musky smell of cedar about him. He must have lain against one for some time before meeting me. Or perhaps this was just his natural smell. Then, there before me: Arlo, putting his cedar-scented palm to my mouth so I would kiss him there and have this smell on my lips.

Seamus burrowed in closer to me as we lay on the cool dirt. In the woods around us the storm was calming itself.

I thought my grief might be so big—and growing, growing—that my body wouldn't be able to contain it. I'd split wide open the way the cedar tree must have when the fire overwhelmed it. Perhaps it had only been his imagination, but when we were miles away from the Preserve, Arlo had said he could still smell the old cedar burning. The scent of it had nearly driven him crazy and he couldn't stop thinking about the cedar being gone from the world. I hope wherever he went, there are cedars.

Seamus got back up in the tight space and turned around three times, then scratched at the dirt and settled again in the same spot where he had started. He curled his body around himself, nose to tail, and kept his eyes on mine to see if I would follow suit. I hadn't slept in so long. I had had a few little naps—the kind that my mother had once called catnaps—over the past three days. But not real sleep. I'd had to be too aware, too alert. The tiniest sound had brought me fully awake, despite being completely exhausted.

But now with Seamus here beside me, with the safety of our little rock hut, despite the hunger twisting my belly and the ache in my head from not eating, despite the pain in my legs from all of the walking after weeks of being contained on that boat, my eyes were so heavy I could barely keep them open.

Seamus gave a couple of weak groans, snuggled in as closely as he could to me, and closed his eyes. I reached out—my arm so heavy—to scratch Seamus's head and the good ole boy stirred only enough to open his eyes and allow his tail to wag once. He was exhausted, too, apparently.

Outside, the rain became softer, a music instead of a cacophony now. The lightning flickered away into unbeing and took the thunder with it. The night gathered in close, shadowing through the woods until it had enclosed all of the trees and rocks, the river and the creek, the sleeping birds, me and the dog.

⚜ ⚜ ⚜

WE WERE AWAKENED by a high, blood-curdling scream.

As soon as I startled awake, I knew it was only the cry of a bird, but I could feel the thump of my heart pounding with fear.

I couldn't believe it: I actually felt rested. "I slept like the dead," my father had always said after a restful night, stretching, his words fitted around a drawn-out yawn. Once again I imagined his dead body drifting in the ocean, and I thought I might be sick. I swallowed the thought down and readied myself for whatever came next. The day was fully bright, so I had slept far past daybreak.

Seamus flopped his tail in the dirt but didn't offer to move until I did. Already he had decided to follow my lead.

"Let's go, little man," I told the dog.

The rock hut was such a good hiding place that I was tempted to stay there to have some peace and quiet for a time, but we had to keep moving. That was the key: keep walking. *Don't give up*, my mother had said. I didn't know what I was walking toward, really. All I knew was one word that was or was not somewhere to walk toward: *Glendalough*. My mother had gone there as a teenager and thought it the most beautiful place she'd ever been. She studied its history and happened upon the theory that it was a thin place. A place protected by positive energy, where the veins of good that ran all throughout the earth intersected. You might laugh at believing in such a thing, but people have fought and died for much more ridiculous beliefs. As soon as she found out that the refugee boats were taking people to Ireland, she had lit upon the idea of Glendalough as a source of hope. She had believed we would be taken into the refugee camps for quarantine and when we got out, we'd live the rest of our days at Glendalough. She had to have something to believe in to get her through.

My only other option was to sit down, which I was not about to do. And if I kept walking, I thought less. Staying still brought up too many memories. The dead, drifting in the sea. My mother, swept away by the waves. My father calling out to me. Charlotte's tiny fingers leaving mine. Arlo's last words: *I'm sorry*. There were too many thoughts swirling in my mind when I was still. They were always present, but if I walked, there were more distractions. If

I kept moving, the grief had a harder time catching up with me.

Seamus stuck nearby, trotting along right next to me. Occasionally he sensed something up ahead and would scamper off to check it out, then come right back. Every once in a while, he was compelled to stop and investigate something, as if he had found an amazing clue to whatever mystery he was intent on solving. But Seamus easily abandoned the finds whenever I stopped and snapped my fingers, saying "Come, boy," in a half whisper, half yell.

We walked for hours in the woods, going up steep hills and then down their other sides, through fern-covered gaps and beneath cliffs that dripped with water. There was water everywhere here: rivers, creeks, bogs, lakes, dripping cliffs. Sometimes I wondered why I kept walking. What use was there? We had thought things would be better in Ireland and there was nothing but desolation. Emptiness. The world had ended. Yet it had not, and as long as there were still cedar trees and dogs, I reckoned I had a reason to keep going.

For long stretches there were no woods and we walked through open pastures again. We hadn't had enough news out of Ireland to know where everyone had gone. It seemed as if they might be dead. Not a single house showed any sign of life, although some weren't in such bad disrepair that they could have stood empty for very long. Others slumped in ruin, desolate with loneliness, or had been burned to the ground. Whatever had taken the people had been recent. We passed swing sets that cheeped their rusty silver sounds in the wind, which was constant in the open fields. We passed plastic sandboxes and short plastic slides and playhouses with tiny doors and windows. But no children or people anywhere to be found. Ireland, it seemed, was an abandoned place except for the soldiers.

I saw a group of them the next morning as I peered out on a wide valley from a hilltop where bees supped at the purple heads of clover. Mist moved in slow stripes across a wide meadow sectioned by stone fences. The soldiers walked in a jagged line, black rifles across their backs, helmets that matched their gray uniforms. The mist was so thick coming up from the river that they appeared and disappeared amid it. I held my breath even though I was well hidden and plenty far enough away. They were moving across the field toward a row of square, squat cars that sat up on the crumbling road, each of them scanning the area around them as if watching for enemies but apparently oblivious to how easily I could have rid the world of each of them if I had had a rifle of my own. I would soon learn exactly who they were so terrified of encountering. They climbed into the brick-shaped cars and drove away, the mist swallowing their vehicles.

The only thing that worried me more than the soldiers was my hunger. My entire life up until this point had been preparing me how to survive. I found enough blackberries to make my hunger pangs pass, but I couldn't get Seamus to eat them. The dog sniffed at them carefully, then turned away as if to say this would not pass muster for him. I found a tree heavy with beechnuts but they weren't ripe yet.

After a long while we came upon the largest group of chanterelles I had ever seen, orange shelves of them twisting around a rotting stump. I broke off as many pieces of the mushroom as I could carry in the pockets of my grimy jeans and inside my shirt. The chanterelles sucked at my skin as I walked. I tried to entice Seamus to eat a few bites, but he merely sniffed at them and turned away. Later I would cook them and see if that might tempt him, I decided.

On and on we went. We saw no other living things apart from the trees, plants, squirrels, and birds. Seamus bolted off after the squirrels, but they were too quick for him. He managed to latch a chipmunk beneath his paw but seemed half-hearted in devouring the tiny thing and it managed to skitter away, too.

Then he stopped suddenly and turned his body to our left, scanning the hillsides. He sniffed at the air with great concern. He raised one leg in that waiting and investigating posture of dogs I would come to know well over the next few days. He ate at the air with his nose in such ferocity that his whole face moved.

"What is it, boy?" I asked, knowing good and well he couldn't answer me. But it felt good to have someone to talk to.

Seamus latched his eyes onto mine in a way that let me know we needed to hide. Now. I don't know how to explain that I knew what the dog meant, but I did. You may think I am out of my mind but that is all right.

I looked away from the hills that he was fixated on again. Yet there was nowhere to hide. I could climb a tree but there was no way I could pull the dog up with me and I wasn't about to leave him.

We were near the edge of a wide, open meadow and the trees were mostly thin and small here, as if they were newer than the rest of the forest. So I ran for the deeper woods, trying to step as lightly as I could. Seamus bounded along beside me. We were both running fast and even in doing I wondered how we'd have the energy to keep going, having eaten so little.

In the deep of the forest, there were massive fallen trees overgrown with the greenest moss I had ever seen. Greener than green, a glowing, otherworldly green that made the woods here feel ancient. Large boulders were covered in the moss, too, and scattered around them, smaller rocks. I plucked up an apple-sized one and kept running. There were large ferns—some as big as chairs—and more rhododendron, but it was not the massive kind we had been in before. This was too spindly for hiding.

But ahead, I saw an enormous beech tree, half hollow and just big enough to hold us. The opening was a few feet up so that it might hide us both if we lay down.

I heard voices behind us, so faint I might have imagined them. But no, there was a man's voice. Then a girl's. The woods carried sound in a strange way, turning normal talk into melodic songs that carried through the tree limbs and slants of light.

I held the rock against my heart.

Louder now.

"Shut your gob!" the man said. "Someone will hear."

Ironic that he might say as much since he was being louder than the girl.

Inside the tree, there was a dirt floor as if it were a little house out in the woods. Seamus stood on his back legs, unable to jump into the safety of the tree. I scooped him up, grabbing him under his front legs. In that moment of heaving him into the tree's hollow, I felt the trust in Seamus's body, the way he relaxed enough to allow me to deposit him into the floor of the hollow tree, the way he had surrendered to me. There was something shattering in that for me, I have to admit.

I became very still, listening.

Nothing.

I couldn't hear the voices anymore. The birds were strangely silent, too, although the day was bright with sunshine, and this was usually the time of day for their loudest conversations.

It was the kind of silence when someone is standing absolutely still and listening. They had heard us or caught a glimpse of us.

The interior of the beech was not as large as I had fancied. The bottom was just big enough to hold Seamus, who had lain down, knowing that he needed to get as low as he could. Even if I had lain atop him, there was not enough room for me to curl up there. I pressed my back against the tree, trying to melt into the trunk to disappear if they came close.

Perhaps they were harmless. Maybe folks who might even be of help. But I couldn't take the chance on it, and Seamus didn't seem to be about to, either.

So we would be still, and wait.

I realized that the two best things I had learned about surviving seemed contradictory, but when done in the proper times, they worked.

The first was to *Keep Moving*, to never give up. This had always been my parents' mantra, usually articulated in the times when neither of them thought they could go on, but somehow always found the strength to do so when they uttered this little sentence, as if the two words themselves supplied energy that kept them moving.

The second was *Be Still*. This was more often something my mother had whispered in times of upset and when we had to hide. Or times when we needed to collect ourselves so that we didn't lose our minds. I remembered her, cooing the words to me. A whisper, really. A prayer. *Be still*. And in its own way this was an instruction on not giving up, too.

A person has to know how to get moving or to calm down. Those two things had served me best in this life.

Maybe this was why the dog and I had a bond from the very beginning. Because we both knew this, in our blood and bones. We knew this above all other things.

I was watching the woods closely, trying to heighten my senses as I had so often done before. There were the same sounds I had come to know about Ireland over the past few days. Small insects clicking in the leaves and brush. A squirrel hopping from one limb to the other, its noise startling in comparison to its smallness. And now I could hear birds, but their chirping was far back in the woods and not nearby. The absence of this noise was disconcerting, as if they were aware of some evil force roaming the hills. A small splash of water; there was a creek somewhere close. But mostly there was quiet. The leaves moved in the breath of a breeze, not enough to make a sound. The light shifted and swayed.

I looked down and saw that Seamus was looking up at me with his strange eyes. Why did this dog trust me? Why had I trusted this dog I'd just met to be on the lookout? Some things cannot be explained.

I looked back up, and there was a man and a girl coming toward us. They were moving with caution, as if walking through neck-high water, the man's right hand out and slightly behind him, as if reminding the girl that she must be silent. They stepped with care, the man's foot landing so gingerly on a branch that it didn't make a sound.

They were both filthy. Both wore large packs on their backs—the girl's so large that I couldn't see how such a small person could bear so much weight. Her hair was such a wild tangle of auburn curls but she pushed it back, hooking locks behind each ear, and I could see her high cheekbones and sharp nose. She was about my age, I figured, but there was something childlike about her in the way she demurred to the man. Then she turned and I could see the right side of her face was covered with a large *B*. Her right eye was in the center of the top round part of the *B*. The man's face had been blackened with soot or ashes for camouflage so I couldn't tell if he was tattooed similarly. He was greasy-haired, wild-eyed. He looked more like a vicious animal than a man. He was a tracker, and a good one; I could tell by how silently he moved, the way he bent to one knee and watched the woods, brought a handful of dirt up to his nose to draw in some scent that only long training could detect. Phoebe had been a tracker, too. The best hunter in our group.

The question was what the man was tracking.

I flattened myself against the tree trunk as much as I could. I could no longer see the man and the girl, but I could still see other parts of the forest. If they moved in just the right way, they'd be able to see me. I held my arm tight to my side to make myself as small as possible, although it would be hard to bring the rock up quickly if I had to. I didn't like the thought of crashing it into the man's temple, but I would if I had to.

And now they were so close that I could hear them, despite their stealth.

I tried to not breathe but this made me want to gasp all the harder. Although the day was mild, I could feel beads of sweat forming on my forehead, trembling on my brow.

At my feet, a growl stirred in Seamus's chest, so low that I could feel it in my feet more than hear it, but still, we couldn't take the chance. I looked down at Seamus, whose eyes were still on mine, and barely shook my head to say, *No, don't do that.*

He quit.

A heavier breeze slunk through the woods, and the leaves moved all around us for a brief moment. Once the wind made its way past, there was total silence again. The people had stopped. I knew they were right beside the beech. Inches away.

Yes. There. I could hear the man's breath. Low. Very quiet. But so close. They were standing next to the tree and something in them knew that we were close. Perhaps the man could smell Seamus just as Seamus could smell him, his nostrils pulsing with sensation at all of the aromas around them.

In one fluid movement, as instant as a match being struck, the man thrust his arm into the hollow of the tree and grabbed hold of me by the neck. Then his grimy face was near mine, stretched wide with a crooked smile.

I tightened my grip on the rock.

"Got you, didn't I?" he said. "Come out of there!"

His bony fingers were miraculously strong, pressing so

hard into my neck that I feared I might pass out. Black spots swam before my eyes with the pain. In his other hand he held a short, wide knife level with my eyes.

He could sense the movement of my arm even before I was about to swing it out. He thrust his fingers into my throat with such might that I was sure I felt the crunch of my windpipe. He lurched forward and I closed my eyes in that half second before he would drive his knife into my eye socket. In that flicker of a moment I not only prepared myself to die but I also welcomed it. I would be folded into the sky.

Then Seamus bolted up out of the trunk below me, hackles raised and a wet growl loud in his throat. Yet still he did not bark. The tracker was so startled that he staggered back with Seamus before him, as threatening as a beagle can be with his arched back and bared teeth. After his initial surprise, however, he grabbed hold of a machete hanging from his belt and sliced it through the air toward Seamus, barely missing his nose.

The girl stood frozen-faced, fading back into the ferns one step at a time, as if she wanted to run away, but there was only so much slack in the rope that tied them together.

I lunged at him with the rock with all the force I could conjure within the confines of the tree. Enough to hit him in the middle of the forehead. He didn't drop the machete, but he lowered it as his free hand went to his face to check for blood. The rock had connected hard enough to daze him but had not broken his skin. As soon as he felt no wetness there, he swung the machete behind him, its wide blade catching a glint of sun that fell through the leaves. And just as he brought it through the air to drive it across Seamus's back, I surged toward him, screaming out "NO," and as I did, the girl drew her walking stick back over her head and plunged the tip of it into the back of his skull. The machete dropped with a dull thud onto the forest floor. He fell onto the ground, too, but he wasn't completely knocked out. Stunned, shaking his head at the blow, but conscious.

I crawled across the ground on all fours to grab hold of Seamus, pulling him farther away from the man. In his blind fury he brought his snout around as if he might bite me, snapping so close I felt his hot breath on the meat above my thumb. Still, he caught himself in time for the teeth to not sink into my hand and his eyes went soft, ashamed.

The girl stood paralyzed, as if in awe of what she had done.

The man pulled himself up to his knees and thrust out one arm to grab hold of the girl by the leg. She let out a jagged scream but didn't fight him. All the while, he kept his eyes on me.

I knew we couldn't leave the girl after she had helped us, but as soon as I looked into her face—smeared with faded greenish mud for camouflage—I knew what she was about to say.

"Run!" she screamed, and we did.

We ran without looking back, out of the woods, all the way across the vast meadow of yellow flowers and briars, jumping across the stone fences, past the complete skeletons of three horses, fording a shallow river whose icy waters only came up to my knees, up a ridge that carried us to the woods ringing the top of a hill. Only here did we stop, panting, trying to catch our breath. I bent and threw up a pitiful string of acrid vomit that still smelled of mushrooms.

As I gathered myself, both hands on the ground in front of me, bent over there in the wilderness all alone, Seamus stood close to my side, waiting for me to gain control again, to be still.

I collapsed on the ground and crawled out to the edge of a small cliff where we could see across the valley. The meadow was empty. They had not followed us.

"We did it, boy," I said, and hooked my arm around the dog's neck. "*You* did it. You saved us." The way Arlo had saved me.

I did not say to him that the girl had saved us, too. That the three of us had worked together. I did not say that we should not have left her there with that man. I did not tell Seamus that I hated to think what he had done to her after we ran.

WE LAY STILL up there among the trees for the next couple of hours, watching the valley between us and the wide woods. The pastures were crisscrossed by crumbling rock walls and hedgerows. From this hill we could see for miles and in the distance, mountains blued the horizon. The day was clear and bright and for a long while I did nothing but watch the shadows of clouds drift over the green grasses below us, trying to not think. I tried to only breathe.

Each time I thought we had waited and watched long enough I would start to get up and Seamus's ears would perk forward at the suggestion that we might be about to move. But I figured that if I thought we had outwaited the tracker down in the woods then he was probably thinking the same thing. So I became still again, watching for a while longer.

Before long, dusk began to spread its quilts out over the land. The time when shadows fall and stillness yawns and stretches its shoulders. A quiet. The birds hushed and all the little live things in the grasses and trees were silent before they began their singing. Crickets and cicadas, katydids and tree frogs. That had always been my favorite time of day. The woods of Ireland were not nearly as loud as those back home, but the soft sounds were a comfort nonetheless. The eastern sky was ablaze with a rich pink that reminded me of watermelon we had had once. Back when gas was still possible to get for normal folks, a traveling grocer had brought it into our town all the way from Kentucky to trade and my mother had given a handful of dried beans for it—an extravagance, but my mother had been unable to deny me the pleasure of tasting it once the man cracked it open there at the market, revealing its perfect ripeness. I remember its thick, hard rind that hid the sweet crispness inside, a taste that made me close my eyes to better concentrate on savoring it.

Everything reminded me of all the people I'd lost.

I decided we couldn't stay here all night, watching for the man. We needed to explore this hill before darkness completely fell.

I reached out to pat Seamus on the head, and he looked up at me appreciatively. When I stood he gave me a concerned look, and then he was padding alongside of me. A sweet-smelling breeze eased past us and gave life to the legion of small leaves decorating the ash and oak trees as we made our way to the summit. Up ahead there was a circle of slender stones, standing on their ends. They were all just a bit taller than me. One of them had fallen over but the rest stood straight. The grass around them swayed in the breeze, a bright green turned golden by the now-violet color of twilight. I had read about Stonehenge and figured these were kin to that way of thinking. No doubt they had stood here for centuries; this had been a holy place visited by tourists but I felt as if I was the first person to see them in a long while. I could only imagine what had once happened here and running my hands over the stones didn't make me any wiser. Once a holy place, always a holy place, I thought. Made all the holier by its loneliness.

Then I saw that what I'd thought were grasses bending lightly in the breeze were actually stems of wild asparagus. We had eaten it quite often back in Maine and the thought of having it again was not appealing, but I needed to eat. The asparagus was much better boiled; I'd have to settle for it raw.

Now I could see that we were surrounded by a complete ring of hazel trees. Back on the Preserve there had been a copse of hazel down by the river, where Phoebe often set up camp to kill deer because the nuts there drew in the most game. My father had told me about the hazel trees. He had had many favorite poets, but he'd loved Yeats above all others and every time we came near the little gathering of hazel trees he had to stop, as a personal tribute to his favorite poet. *I went out to the hazel wood / Because a fire was in my head*, he'd whisper. Each time he told me about the power hazel trees possessed. How they offered protection to those who acknowledged them.

"Let's make camp here tonight," I told Seamus, and went about gathering kindling so we could build a fire once darkness had control of the land again.

Seamus stayed close to my heels as I picked up branches. There was still enough light to see but darkness was easing in. I caught sight of a slender, well-traveled animal path and followed it. Seamus found fox scat in the middle of the trail and was drawing in great breaths of it when I squatted to identify it the way Phoebe had taught me. After smelling it properly, Seamus promptly swallowed the blackened turds whole, causing my stomach to lurch. He licked his lips, completely without shame.

We followed the path past the hazel trees, back beyond the ash and oak to a hillside that held exactly what I had suspected, wet ground, which meant one thing: a spring.

There was a patch of lush green grass and small trees heavy with pink flowers that quivered in twilight's dying breaths. I stepped into the swampy ground and listened. There it was, the gurgle of a spring. Seamus darted into the hillside and lapped at the water, and I saw where the trickle barely showed itself among a tangle of honeysuckle vines and mossy rocks. We both drank our fill. The water was rich with the taste of minerals.

As night purpled the sky I roasted mushrooms on heated rocks pushed into the fire and managed to get Seamus to eat a handful of them once they had cooled. Maybe he thought they were meat. Or maybe he finally had succumbed to hunger.

Although there was a comfort in sitting close to the crackling flames, the orange light exposed our position, making us visible from a long way off. I couldn't hardly enjoy the solace or warmth because I was constantly looking out into the darkness. Only the presence of the hazel trees around me and the knowledge that Seamus was here and on alert allowed me the peace of mind to drift off to sleep. We lay right in the middle of the circle of stones and ring of hazel trees by the fire. Seamus, as had become his habit, lay against me.

I couldn't imagine how we had all gone so long without dogs. My parents had told me enough about dogs for me to know that most of them were good like Seamus, that they had once been called people's best friends. My parents had told me how the world had dulled and hardened when the dogs had disappeared in the early days of the war. Many people had thought it a humane thing to put them down, saving them from starving in the streets. I suspected I knew what had happened to many more of them, but I didn't want to think about that. The lack of dogs was something that had troubled my father. More than once, he had told me he always pictured me growing up with a dog, the way he had. He had shown me photos of the dogs of his childhood. A fluffy white spitz named Fala, a strong-chested mutt named Rufus; I remembered them even though I had never known them. When I was little, I had looked through those photos the way some little kids have a favorite picture book. I had to sneak because the photos were so valuable. By the time we got to Nova Scotia my mother had whittled her pack of photos down to about a dozen she kept rubber-banded in the duffel. Now the duffel and everything we had had was on the bottom of the sea off the coast of Ireland, along with the only photographs of any of us.

I wouldn't think about that, though. I decided I would think only of Seamus there beside me. I'd study on how good he was, and how he made me feel safe and not so alone in the world. The steady rise and fall of his chest, the rat-a-tat of his little fast heart. The way he knew to keep watch so I could sleep.

And then: rest.

I awoke to find Seamus staring out into the night with his ears perked up. I heard him growl quietly and then I managed to go back to sleep. But the second time I felt that hum of alarm, I jumped up, ready for whatever was coming for us. The fire had died and grown cold by now—there was only the faintest glow of pulsing embers at its center—so at least we weren't easy to see. I walked the perimeter of the stones, peering out into the shadows in a cold sweat. I saw nothing more than the still leaves of the hazel trees. There was not one sound, as if this little hill was cut off from the rest of the world completely—no birds, none of the little live things, not even a breeze.

I slept again for a couple of hours, riddled by dreams that made me awake feeling grief-stricken. Arlo's lips on mine. Then, Arlo alive but still buried beneath all of those rocks back in Canada. My father, in golden light, running his hand along the trunks of birch trees. My mother, floating facedown, eyes open.

At long last daylight touched my eyelids and nudged me awake. Above, the sky groaned open with a heavy grayness and the scent of rain on the air. Seamus was dozing beside me, but as soon as I rose up his eyes opened and he spread his mouth in a wide yawn, his tongue curling up to brush the roof of his mouth, as he stretched. He was surprised by the involuntary yelp in the back of his throat. This was the only real sound I had heard come from him so far. I gave his head a good rub and stood up, and he studied me, then hopped up to follow close behind me.

A large branch had fallen from the hazel tree. This would make a good walking stick and maybe some of the protection the hazel offered would go along with us. I doubted the existence of magic, but not enough to completely deny the fact that it might exist. If anything in this world was holy it was a tree. This much I knew for sure.

We walked back out to the cliffs where we had lain yesterday to watch the valley. Below us a white mist moved across the pastures. The blue mountains in the east I had seen yesterday were hidden by a white haze. Still, I knew they were there. And that was where we were headed.

THE MORNING THAT changed everything, I was thinking of the song "The Lark Ascending" while we walked. Phoebe had played it for us on her fiddle sometimes in the evenings while we sat around the fire, back home on the Preserve. The high, lonesome notes of "The Lark Ascending" conjured up grief in me long before I really knew what that was. Before I lost everything, when I was just a little boy and had all the people I loved the most with me.

"This one's for you," Phoebe had always said. My mother hadn't known the song when she'd named me—she just liked the way *Lark* sounded. But it had become Phoebe's song for me. My father said it had been inspired by a poem, but he couldn't spout any lines from it. Still, the tune was hard to get out of your head. The song sounded like an adventure about to happen even while it mourned for some past that was being left behind. That was the way the light fell greenly through the leaves that morning, the way the cool air felt on my face. I had loved to watch Phoebe play that song, her eyes closed and her cheek perched upon the fiddle as if they were two parts of a whole, as if the fiddle was playing her, as if she'd fallen asleep against it and had allowed it to take control of her.

For a time we walked alongside a paved road that looked more modern than anything we had seen. There was a white line down the middle, and instead of hedgerows close on either side, there were wide concrete shoulders. There were a few trees along the road but not much else to hide us from anyone who might be atop one of the hills on either side of us, watching. But we had no other choice; there were no woods here.

We came to a squat stone church with a short steeple topped by a cross. The blue door of the church was hanging from only one hinge and quivered there in the shadowy doorway each time the wind found it. Just past the church was a walled cemetery full of white gravestones, each with a small concrete wall around its perimeter. In one corner was a small grove of cedars crowding around a life-size crucifixion scene.

I looked behind the church, where a green mountain rose, and I spotted a thin column of smoke twisting its way up on the sky near the mountain's summit. Besides the

soldiers and the man and girl in the woods, this was the
only evidence of living people since I had arrived on this
forsaken island.

A trio of birds burst out of the cedars to my left, drawing my eye to the other side of the short wall. And there was
a huge pile of dirt that looked as if it had only recently been
dug. Around the edges of the mound were several crosses
made of rough branches tied together with old belts or pieces
of rope. There were also square pieces of thin wood with
names burned into them. On the largest one was written:

> This is the mass grave
> of the 49 victims
> of the Slieve Séipéal Massacre,
> murdered by the Black Fox.
> Never forget.

Of course everyone now knows about what happened to
the good people of Slieve Séipéal. But back then word of it
had not made its way much past this little village. A chill
ran through me. A wind came down out of the mountain,
sweet with the scent of pine trees, oaky with wood smoke. I
clicked my tongue so Seamus would follow. We moved on,
the dog and me.

WE TOOK OFF across the field toward a grove of trees between the church and the mountain so we'd have some cover. I kept my eye on the finger of blue smoke drifting up from the far mountain—thinner now, so thin that I may not have been able to spot it at all had I not seen it before.

The grove was slender and stretched as far as I could see, which meant the trees were most likely lining a creek or river. I spotted a thin metal wire running from the ground and up into a massive beech tree. I didn't know what it was, and I wasn't about to find out. I called out to Seamus so he wouldn't go near it and from there on out we stayed at the very edge of the tree line, just enough to be hidden.

We walked until I couldn't go any farther. My lack of sleep from the night before had nearly done me in and we had come upon an ancient oak tree whose broad limbs were perfectly situated for me to climb up and have a nap without fear of falling out. Seamus didn't like being left alone below but I knew that he'd curl up at the base of the tree to wait for me to rise again. I propped my hazel stick against the trunk and clambered up.

I slept a dreamless sleep for what must have been a solid two hours because the sky had dimmed and lowered by the time I awoke. Evening had fallen. As soon as I jumped down, Seamus took off across the field. I yelled for him to wait, but he was gone, all four legs pumping and his head set low against the wind. I didn't want to lose him. I grabbed my stick and ran as fast as I could, hoping I could keep up.

I managed to keep my eye on Seamus enough to follow and when I found him I collapsed, desperate for breath. He was hunkered low in the ferns at the edge of a clearing.

I dropped to all fours and crawled up beside him. I looked out to the clearing and saw a small stone house and a yard, golden with long, thin grass. The side of the house facing us was lit a comforting orange from a little fire that was burning near it, although the fire itself was out of our sight. I caught the savory aroma of meat and my mouth watered. I had not had meat since long before crossing the ocean, since we'd eaten the last of our deer jerky while walking to Nova Scotia.

Then I heard a woman, singing.

The water is wide, I cannot cross over
Neither have I wings to fly
Give me a boat that can carry two
And both shall cross, my true love and I

Her voice was high and clear but strong, too. Determined sounding, as if she were singing loud like this to defy anyone who might be aiming to harm her. But there was some kind of hope in her singing, too. The way Miriam had sounded during the crossing. The way Phoebe's fiddle had sounded when it wasn't crying out a sadness.

Seamus clearly smelled the meat. His eyes were locked on the house as if figuring out how he might snatch the meat and make a clean getaway.

"No, buddy," I said, curling two fingers beneath Seamus's red collar, but I wasn't strong enough. He was gone, vaulting from the cover of the woods and bounding across the grass with amazing speed.

I ran after him and as I came over a small rise, I saw a woman sitting by the fire, her face lit golden by the flames, her eyes closed as she sang. A metal rod hung over the fire with a small roast glistening there. But no sooner than I had seen her, she opened her eyes to Seamus heading straight for her. She launched to her feet, bringing a metal pipe up in the stance of someone who knew how to use it. Just as he reached the fire she swung it through the air.

"No!" I let loose the scream before I knew I was going to open my mouth.

The woman had not hit him but the slice of the pipe through the air had kept Seamus back, and now they stood on opposite sides of the fire, considering each other. Still Seamus did not bark nor make a sound. He simply eyed the roast.

"Who's there?" the woman yelled. "Come out where I can see you! Come on, then. Let's get this over with."

There was not a sound, not even a cricket cheeping.

The woman looked from Seamus and back to the woods. She couldn't see me.

"There's a gun pointed right on you from inside the house!" She was taking a different tactic now. "Come out or he'll open fire!"

Seamus made a leap for the food and the woman brought the pipe around, nearly connecting with Seamus's head but she missed.

I ran toward the fire, although as soon as I started moving I thought how stupid I was as I had no way of knowing if there was a scope trained on me or not. Ever since the shots had rung out to kill Sera and Arlo, I had imagined a gun aiming at me from a distance. But in that half-second before my right foot took off, I knew that I couldn't lose Seamus. No. Not after everyone else.

Seamus had run beneath the small back porch of the house and I panicked, realizing then that I was completely in the open yard.

"Stop," the woman yelled, stepping forward with the pipe poised to cave in my skull. She was wearing fingerless

gloves and a green canvas jacket with four pockets, two
near her shoulders and two where it struck her waist. "Drop
that stick!"

I hadn't even realized I was still hanging on to my hazel
limb, and I let it fall to the ground.

"Put your hands up and come here."

I moved my arms into the air but didn't step forward.

"I just want my dog," I said. "Let me have him and we'll
go."

Behind her I could see Seamus crawling out from under
the edge of the porch, making sure she wasn't going to harm
me. He had latched his eyes right on her and I thought he
might spring at her.

"I won't hurt you," she said, just as I had said to Seamus
when we first met. She put her hand up to her mouth.
"You're just a lad, then," she said, more like five exhala-
tions than five words.

"I'm twenty years old."

"You don't look it," she said, eyeing me with suspicion.

"Well, I am."

"All right then," she said, and poked at the fire with the
metal pipe. "Doesn't matter anyway, does it?" I couldn't
imagine the person who possessed that sad, high voice
being mean. As she came closer, I could see her better: She
was very slender and her face was square with high cheekbones. Her black hair swept back to reveal a clever, lined
forehead. Even in the dark I could see the strange blueness

of her eyes, blue like pictures of the Caribbean I had seen in books from Before. She must have been a few years older than my mother.

"Are you hurt?"

"No."

"Are you alone?"

I nodded. Seamus eased out from under the porch.

"Why are you here?" she asked.

"Our boat was sunk, and I'm trying to reach a place called Glendalough."

"You sound like an American."

I nodded again. Seamus had scooted around so that his rump rested atop my foot.

"How long have you been here?" she asked.

"Three days."

"Are you starving?" she asked.

I shook my head, no, although in retrospect this was a strange thing to do since my belly had more or less been mewing with hunger since we had left our cabin back in Maine. "He smelled the meat. We were in the woods, and he smelled it and I couldn't make him stop."

"Do you have any other weapons?"

I shook my head, no.

"That's a bit silly of you, then," she said. She eased toward me, pipe held up. "I'll need to check for that if you want to come in here. Otherwise, turn around and leave now."

I was so weary. I just wanted to talk to another person. Some part of me no longer cared what happened, even if my parents' prodding to stay in motion never left my mind. I put my arms up, an invitation for her to do whatever she needed to do.

"If you try anything I will beat your brains out," she said. "I won't hesitate to kill you. I've done it before."

I saw her story on her face, and it was not a happy or tender one. Life had left its mark on her, even if it couldn't completely put out the way her face shone. She approached me like someone encountering a wild animal and Seamus's hackles rose. A growl boiled in the back of his throat. I rubbed him behind the ears and told him it was okay and after a moment he relented. She propped the pipe on her shoulder as she patted me down with one hand.

She stood back and lowered the pipe, the knuckles of one fist on her left hip. "Okay, we'll give it a go, then, will we? At this point there's nothing left to lose," she said, as if reading my mind. I thought she was talking to herself out of habit more than speaking to me. She put out her hand. "I'm called Helen. Come on then," she said, and I knew this meant to shake her hand, so I did, with some amount of trepidation, and told her my name.

"Come here, sit by the fire," she said. "Come and eat."

"I THOUGHT THEY were all gone," Helen said, nodding to Seamus. She had barely stopped talking since we'd settled in next to the fire. She didn't stop even as she daintily ate the rabbit she had cooked. She had thrown Seamus the rabbit's guts in a high arc and he had slurped them down with much noise and commotion. "Everyone did away with them, you see. As a precaution in case there were food shortages. And there were, of course. The same thing happened in England during World War II. They killed their pets to spare them starving or being eaten."

I was glad I had finished my food. I didn't respond, desperate to not even think about such a thing.

"There were two things from the beginning I can't get over. The dogs and the babies being gone. Back when they first closed the borders and the English took over again, in our weakest moment," she said, "they sterilized half the women. To keep the population low so the food would last longer, they said. By a random lottery, they said. Which is a farce because they sterilized the lower classes only. As it always is. It was either take the sterilization injection or be taken off to the camps. Isn't that the way of the world, then?" she asked. I could tell by her tone that she did not really expect an answer.

I had told her the brief version of everything that had happened to me, too. I did not elaborate on any of it. I told her the crossing was misery, that my father had slipped into the sea with a sound as equally small as the infant's body. I told her about the ship sinking, my mother drowning. Everyone dead. I told her about my day of delirium on the beach. I did not mention Arlo. I couldn't say it out loud yet. I didn't tell her about Phoebe and Sera, or about our holy days on the mountain in Maine in between our tragedies.

"But how did you make it past the border guards?"

"They thought we were all dead, I guess. They left. I saw other patrols on my way here, but I managed to hide from them."

"Oh, lad, you've been through such a terrible ordeal, haven't you?" She looked at me with such sadness as she ate some chanterelles. I had contributed those to the meal and Helen had produced a bottle containing some kind of oil and a little tin where she sautéed them. They were almost as tasty as the rabbit.

"How could they refuse people who had been through what we've been through?"

"At least I can be proud of Ireland for being the last one to take in refugees, the last one to—"

"What do you mean? They sank our boat. They meant to kill us."

"But those were not the Irish," Helen said, her eyes large and completely on my face again. "When the Nays started to take over the UK, England left us on our own. They wanted to stop us from letting anyone in because their main goal is to rid Ireland and all of the UK of immigrants. Of course the Nays hate Catholics about as much as they hate Muslims and Jews. But the Nays—they're the ones sinking the refugee boats, love."

"What are they?"

"A faction of fools playing soldier, but they have help from outside forces. Nobody knows who, exactly. Called the Nays because they say no to everything. Immigrants in particular, especially black and brown ones. They've been brewing for decades, just waiting for some catastrophe like we've all been through so they could rise to power. And now they have."

"The Fundies waited for their perfect moment, too," I said.

She nodded. "At first the Nays forced the boats to stay out on the water. Hundreds of people starved to death out there. But when they began to fear these boats might be coming to help us fight back, they started firing on them, setting the mines. All of it is murder. But we're fighting back."

"Fighting back?" I had seen patrols, but no fighting, as if the whole country had given up.

"Of course. We Irish have had to fight to survive ever since time began." She took more of the mushrooms, swallowing before she even had time to taste them. "A few months ago, all of West Cork was ground zero, but the Resistance has pushed them back. The front lines are north of us by a hundred miles. America may be no more, but Ireland still has a fighting chance."

"So the soldiers I saw were the Resistance."

"No," she said, around a laugh the length of her single word. "You'll not see the Resistance in a group like that. Just because the Nays have been pushed back doesn't mean we're rid of them. They still control the coasts and they still come through here to reach it. But mostly these are desolate lands, now, and this used to be the prettiest place on earth."

I thought of our mountain in Maine.

"And there's no running water or electricity. I reckon the Nays cut it, to make it harder for us to fight back. Everyone is dead, or they left, or were rounded up. I'm all alone in the world now."

"But who is the Resistance?"

"Just normal Irish folk. Trying to save our country. Once again."

"Are you one of those fighting back?"

Helen looked at me and lifted her chin. I took that as a yes.

"Before all of this more than three-quarters of the pop-ulation died in the famine. Now West Cork is a few peo-ple hiding out in the countryside and everyone else in the walled cities: Cork, Galway, Limerick, Dublin, Belfast. They were told they were being taken there to be protected, but they're prisoners."

Seamus had been busy licking the spot where Helen had thrown the guts. Now he came and put his head against Helen's leg to be petted. She ran both her thumbs up his snout, massaging over his eyes. "A good auld man he is," Helen said. "What do you call him?"

"Seamus."

"For the poet, I'm supposing."

I thought of my father by the fire back home.

"It was on his tag when I found him."

Helen scratched Seamus behind his ears—one hand atop each ear—and the dog rolled his eyes back in his head in delight, causing us to laugh together. A knife of guilt sliced through me. I couldn't remember the last time I had laughed. Most likely back when we were walking to Nova Scotia. Certainly not since Arlo had died. I had not laughed, not one time, during the crossing.

"He's a beagle," I said, although she was plenty old to remember dogs, much better than I could.

"They're such good dogs. Sweet, gentle. Very loyal," she said, and stopped petting Seamus all at once. Her brow wrinkled and she brought her hands to her face. "I had forgotten. How good they are. Dogs."

"I was little when they were taken away back home."

"That's the scary thing, isn't it? That we can so easily forget."

A silence fell between us, and I looked out toward the woods where we had walked earlier. The Irish night had settled in its shadowy way.

"The strangest thing is that he hasn't barked one time since I found him," I said. "In books dogs are all the time barking."

"Yes, that's unheard of." She moved his face around in her hands so that his eyes rolled back in pleasure again. "I'm guessing his silence enabled him to hide. Perhaps his last owner trained him to not bark. Which would be no small feat with a beagle. They're notorious for being loud." She laughed to herself. "That's what I mean. We forget things like that. The sound of barking."

"I never knew the sound to begin with."

"You're the first person I've talked to in two years," she said. "Not another soul."

"How could that be?"

"We lived in West Cork. Everyone we knew either died in the famine or was hauled off or killed for one reason or another. One by one there was nobody left but me and my husband in our village. First the food shortages after so many crops were destroyed around the world. Then so many rounded up. So many others who left to get away from the warfare. But one of the things that haunts me most is when we had to get rid of the dogs. My husband took ours away. Fitz, he was called. The dog, I mean."

"To where?"

"I expect he took him into the woods and shot him. It was a hard thing, but necessary. Better than to turn them out and let them starve." Her words were matter-of-fact, but her face was not. She had paled, and before she spoke her mouth gathered and she clenched her jaw, revealing the square bone there. "I told him I didn't want to know. Ever."

"What happened to your husband?" I asked.

"He went to the sea, to find food. Two years ago. And I never saw him again. I waited nineteen months, but then the Nays settled in our village, so I had to start moving. And I haven't stopped since." Helen picked up a branch and poked at the fire, giving it enough air so that flames sizzled into being between the logs. "Moving in circles, mostly. As far as I can figure out, we're only a couple days' walk from West Cork right now. So I surely haven't gotten far in a half year's time. But there's nowhere to go but round and round."

"Everybody I ever knew is dead, too."

"We are orphans each one, I reckon," she said. The orange flames of the fire caught in her eyes when she looked up at me. "Me, you, and the good auld dog."

Helen watched the fire for a time while she petted

Seamus. He lay very still, head atop his front paws, with sleepy eyes.

"Have you heard of a place called Glendalough?" I asked.

"Of course. It's an old monastic settlement, right in the middle of the Wicklow Mountains. Some people say it is a thin place."

"That's where my mother intended to take us. She said it was the place of a spiritual vortex. Do you know what that is?"

"Where the veil is thinner between this world and some other one. I've heard of folks who think that going to the vortexes are the only safe places left. It's hocus-pocus, though, love."

"My parents weren't people who believed in nonsense," I said, feeling as if I had to come to their defense. I remembered my father reciting Yeats one night to us: *The world is full of magic things, patiently waiting for our senses to grow sharper.*

Helen didn't seem bothered that she might have been offensive. "I used to believe very hard. In all of it. In people. In karma. I used to go to Mass without fail, even after it was outlawed. We'd go to the old holy wells to worship, like they had to do in the old days. Risked our lives. For what? For who? No one. Nothing." A log fell in the fire, sending a column of red sparks into the air. "After all that has happened, I only believe in myself. That's all it pays a person to believe in, you see. And you ought to do the same."

"I do," I said, not sounding very convincing.

She leaned forward and looked up to lock her eyes on mine. "I'm not intending to be cold-hearted. But it's the way of the world now, lad."

I knew exactly what she meant. But I had to go on believing in something. I didn't know what exactly. A mystery. That's what it was. Some people called the mystery love and some people called it God. I didn't know its name, but I knew there was something, even if it was unknowable. I had lost everyone I had ever cared about. I needed something to be tethered to, or some way of feeling like I could speak to everyone I'd lost.

"Why do they think Glendalough is special?"

Helen let out a long sigh as if the thought of telling this exhausted her. "Some people say that there are energy fields in particular places, and lines that connect them. Ley lines. When the ley lines cross, there are hot spots of energy. Spiritual vortexes, thin places: all one and the same. And these are like magnets that can align spiritual properties instead of material ones. Some think it's because of mineral deposits whose power we don't completely understand, or something even more supernatural. Folks think that's why the old priest went to Glendalough to begin with, drawn there without knowing why. There's a Heaney poem about the priest praying for so long with his arms stretched out that a blackbird builds a nest in his hand," she said while she moved her knuckles around the top of Seamus's head. "I just think that some places feel better than others, a perfect storm of good things merging. They're safe places, where you feel better just because of where you are. And when people feel good, they're better to one another, so they become safe places, too."

The idea of a safe place felt magical enough to me.

"Have you heard any news from America?"

She shook her head. "Not in ages. All I know is that the fires and the famine happened and that the Fundamentalists took control. And I know the refugees were pouring into Ireland, claiming sanctuary."

"So many died after the crops were destroyed, I can't even imagine how many," I said. "Once the fires came nearer and the Fundies were in control, we knew we had to leave."

"The strangest part is how quickly it all went backward," Helen said. "All during my youth there were steps forward. The day that gay marriage was legalized we danced in the streets of Cork. There are always bigots pushing against it, of course. But gains. Steps forward in my lifetime I would have never believed," she said. "And then, well, here we are. Moving backwards. History repeats itself."

"That's what my father always said."

"Zealots are always ready to take over. No one ever thought it could happen here, but we were overestimating human beings. Turns out it's easy to convert more people to a cause that takes power from others, that thrives on meanness."

I nodded. "We all went into hiding after that."

"Where did you hide?"

"Up in the mountains. In Maine."

"That's near Canada, isn't it?"

I nodded.

"And how was that?"

I saw my father splitting wood. My mother coming back with a stringer heavy with squirrels. A thin smoke coming from the chimney of our cabin. Arlo. Always Arlo. He stood in the swimming hole with water lapping at his hips. He looked over his shoulder at me as we ran down the path. He held a sugar maple leaf up to the sunlight so he could study its veins. For two years we were a couple in our own little home, and nobody bothered us.

"We did just fine," I told her. But I wanted to say: it was Paradise. I wanted to say: if only we could go back to that time and that place. But there was no going back. There was no home for me anywhere in the world. I was running for my life, trying to find a home in a country that didn't want me. Home had once been our town we had left back in Maryland when I was little. For the longest time home had been our mountain in Maine, where we had been completely free. But more than anything, home was my people. Now that they were gone, I had nothing. No country. No people. Only myself. Unwanted, alone, not alive so much as simply surviving. I had to try to not linger too much on these thoughts or they would conjure a weight of defeat in me too heavy to carry. I would not be able to keep going if I allowed myself to think this way too much.

In the woods there was a great splintering sound like a tree cracking wide open. Helen rose up and gripped the metal pipe instantly. Seamus stood at attention, his ears forward, his eyes focused on the darkening woods.

"Get away from the fire!" Helen whispered. "They might see us."

I obeyed, slinking into the shadows with my back flat against the house, and slid down to the ground. Only Seamus stayed lit by the fire, easily seen by anyone out in the nighttime.

"Seamus, come," I hissed. "Come here, boy."

Seamus turned toward my voice but then looked back to the woods. He did not bark but there was a growl deep in the back of his throat. Before I had heard only a little hum coming from his belly, but now he sounded a true alarm.

I could hear Helen scratching and digging. Then suddenly she dashed a bucket of dirt onto the fire—the curve of soil arching through the air—extinguishing all but the embers instantly. The darkness around us was sudden and complete.

"You've led someone to us," she said.

"No, I watched to make sure no one was following us."

My eyes took a moment to adjust before I could see her. Purple clouds had eased over the moon, causing the night to thicken.

"Who is it?" I whispered to her.

"The Banished, I'd say. They're always sneaking about trying to steal what they can. They often won't only steal from a person, they'll also kill them. Even when they don't have to. Or worse."

I thought of the man and the girl. The Banished. That name fit the way they had looked: alone, wandering, desperate, relentless. But I wasn't about to tell her about them for fear she'd run me off for leading them to her. "Why were they banished? By who?"

"They were originally part of the rebel forces, but they sold rebel secrets to the Nays. Anyone suspected of being a traitor was tattooed by the rebels on the face, not only to warn other rebels but also so the Nays can't use them anymore." Here she drew a *B* over her face. "A big B. Marked so they can't be mistaken, rejected by everyone."

"But maybe it's the Nays, patrolling," I said.

"The patrols don't hide. They march right in, guns drawn."

"But what was that sound?"

"One of my traps," she said, calmly.

"What kind of trap?"

"A way for me to stay safe."

"Do the traps kill people?"

"Not usually. Sometimes. It might have only been tripped."

We stayed still and silent for at least an hour before either of us spoke again. Years of fear had taught me what I had to do. In that hour I began to feel so low that I thought I might not be able to come back out of it again. I kept feeling my father's hand on my back, moving in that comforting, perfect circle. *Be still*, the circle told me. *Go*, my mother whispered in my right ear.

But she was not there. Nor was my father. There was only this woman I didn't know, and Seamus. At least there was Seamus, who had finally come to lean against my leg. He was resting there now, although he had not given up watching the woods, and so I thought there must have been someone still out there. If it had just been a falling limb or some natural moaning of the forest, Seamus would have relaxed by now. Who knew if it was a person or an animal. I could only hope for the latter.

"Lark?" Helen whispered. She was closer than I had thought. "Have you fallen asleep?"

"No."

"Well, you ought to. I'll keep watch. It's hours yet until morning."

"There's something out there. I can tell by how Seamus is acting."

"I think so, too," she said. "I can feel it."

"Do patrols often come through here?"

"How should I know?" she answered. "I'm travel-ing through myself, just like you. It doesn't pay to be still nowadays."

"This isn't your house?"

"Of course not," she said.

"Where were you headed?" I whispered. There was something comforting about talking in the darkness like this, unable to see one another, this communion of words between two people in hiding.

"Go on to sleep, now, Lark," she said, after a long pause. "Go on to sleep and in the morning, we'll move on."

Seamus burrowed in closer to me and gave one of his little deep-throated grunts that meant he was settling. He had decided to let Helen keep watch, so I reckoned I should trust her as well. She could slash my throat in the middle of the night but what good would that do her? I had noth-ing she would want to take. I pushed the distrust and fear away. I pushed the voices and faces of my parents out of my mind. I focused on the darkness behind my eyelids—a dark darker than black—and before I knew it, I had found sleep.

SEAMUS DREAMS OF the island when he sleeps. He dreams
of chasing the gulls. In his dreams there is the sound of the
sea—the endless, relentless, eternal crashing of the waves
upon the black rocks, the smooth kiss of the water on the
sandy beach. He dreams of the clicks and crunch of driftwood between his teeth. He sees the cows eyeing him with
suspicion, the low moos they cooed to him on cool mornings when the air was so damp that he could see the tiny
droplets like rain in front of his eyes. He pictures the man
reaching down to scratch his head. In his sleep he can feel
this, the joy of it, the comfort.

He dreams of feeling safe.

Most of all Seamus dreams of when he and the man
had the island all to themselves and they climbed way up

to the highest cliffs. The clean smell of the salty air. The green taste of the grass. The sound of the crashing waves and the breeze in the grasses. How they lay upon the grass in patches of sunshine and the man reached over to run his hand down the length of him. The warmth of the sun on his haunch. When he rose, he found water spilling from the man's eyes down his cheeks.

In his sleep he runs alongside the man on the way back home. Back when he could still bark. When he could still let loose and set it out onto the air for others to hear. In his dreams he remembers all of it: the way it all looked, smelled, sounded, tasted, and oh, best of all, the way it felt.

IN THE BLUEST part of the night Seamus startles awake but only opens his eyes; he doesn't move anything else for a moment as he takes in the quiet. He takes a deep draw of the air: the musk of a fox spying from somewhere nearby; the sweet smell of the spot where the rabbit guts hit the ground, although he was sure he licked that clean; the dark aroma of the ashes, which causes him to notice his thirst. There is only the soft sound of the young man breathing beside him. He looks out toward the field and the wood. He can see the black figures of trees against the sky, which is gray and blue at the same time.

Seamus moves his head with caution—he doesn't want to draw any attention to himself—and there is the woman, looking out at the field and the wood as well. Her mouth is

set in a firm line, and she doesn't blink often. She is thinking about something very hard.

He should go to her, but he doesn't dare move. He wants
to study her awhile more. She has ahold of the metal pipe
with both hands and it is resting on the ground between her
legs. Every once in a while, she looks down as if it might
have moved, then she taps its end against the ground to
make a low sound that is more of a vibration than anything
else. Seamus can feel it singing in his ears and chest each
time she does this.

He looks to the young man's face, which is very close to
his own. Right now the young man has his arm wrapped
around Seamus and his face is like the sea on a calm day.
Seamus is just fine with that as it feels good for someone to
hold on to him. Only when the young man sleeps does he
not look worried. Only when he sleeps is he not in motion.
He is always wanting to keep moving. "Come on, boy," he
says every time Seamus pauses too long over a good scent or
just wants to sit and let the breeze wash over him.

"Hello, sweet auld man," the woman says, and her
voice matches her face in its sadness. "What a good soul
you are."

He wags his tail a couple times to let her know he
likes her.

"Do you know what I am, then, good madra? Have ye
figured it all out?"

Seamus perks his ears and lets his tail flop three more

times. She turns her face back toward the field and the wood to keep watch. He considers ambling over to lick at the rabbit guts spot again, but he feels too good where he's lying, so he doesn't. After a time, he is lulled back to sleep by the young man's breathing, by the thump of his heart against him.

⚓ ⚓ ⚓

A HARD KICK to the bottom of my shoe and there was sunlight, sudden and white, blinding me. The instant sound
of morning birdcall, a breeze running through the leaves.
Seamus licking at my face, already up and about and ready
to start his day. And Helen, standing over me, looking completely refreshed although she must not have slept at all. In
the morning light I was able to see a deep scar that ran from
her jawbone down to her neck, disappearing into her collar.
Her hair had been cut so that one side hung slightly lower
than the other. I imagined her sawing away at her locks
with a butcher knife.

"Let's get moving," Helen said. "I don't stay still once
it's full morning." She attached a knife sheath to her belt.
"Either come now or you can go on your own."

"Where?"

"You have me thinking about Glendalough. The Wicklow Mountains might offer more protection. Better than roaming in circles like I've been doing."

Helen was hanging a strap over her shoulders. A rifle was attached to the broad green band.

"You have a *gun*?" Back home only the Fundies had firearms. They had always been loudest about making sure there was no gun control until they controlled them all.

Helen nodded. "And look what else."

She held forth her hand, revealing two small tan eggs dotted with brown on her palm. "They've been boiled." She fished into the pocket of her jacket with her free hand and produced a glass shaker of salt. "And look here, wonder of wonders."

"But how?"

"There's an abandoned quail farm a day's walk from here and some of the quail still live out along the River Bride. I gathered two dozen and boiled them up. They'll keep for a while."

I peeled the eggs and their whiteness glowed against my dirty palm before I bit into one and the rich taste of the yolk exploded on my tongue. I couldn't remember the last time I had tasted something so delicious. Helen kicked the bottom of my shoe again.

"Come on, let's see what's in those woods."

"Why didn't you use the gun last night?"

"And do what, shoot up the woods? I save the bullets to use on the drones."

"You shoot down drones?"

She bunched her eyebrows together as if this was a ridiculous question. "Of course."

Then she turned on one heel and strode across the field. Seamus trotted alongside her and glanced back to make sure I was going to join them.

"Grab that knapsack," Helen called out without turning around, and I picked up the green bag from the ground and hurried behind her. She seemed to have decided that the three of us were a team now. All I could do was trust my instinct that she was good. Seamus and I had slept while she watched over us. She had given us food. Maybe she was one of the patrols, rounding people up, but I'd take my chances.

Helen was stronger than I had first reckoned. Fiercer. The orange glow of the fire had softened her face last night. She was much harder than I had first thought. There were deep lines at her eyes and around her mouth. She moved in a slinking sort of motion, more like a fox than a person. I was having trouble keeping up with her.

A flurry of small white moths came circling up out of the long grasses and Seamus lunged for them, snapping his teeth together to catch them in his mouth. They easily dodged him, twisting away along the feathery tufts at the tops of grass.

"They could still be watching us," Helen said without turning to face me. Now I saw that she was holding the rifle firmly in both hands: her right hand gripping near the trigger and her left steadying the barrel. She was looking up at the sky—for drones, apparently—and then straight ahead, scanning the trees in the thick forest for any sign of life. "Hurry up so we're not out in the open."

A host of starlings sprang from the high branches of a pine tree, causing both of us to hunker down and scamper across the remaining bit of field until we were within the cover of forest. Seamus turned in a circle at our feet, his nose to the ground as if suddenly picking up a ripe scent, then zoomed ahead of us, and Helen followed, motioning for me to do so as well.

"He's moving in a straight line," she whispered.

"So?"

"Animals rarely move in a straight line. He's smelling a person."

As soon as we got in the woods we could see the long metal wire, like the one I'd seen a few days before, dangling from a broken tree branch. It must have been a complicated concoction, half tripwire and half assault-by-tree. When the wire was tripped, a limb would swing down and knock them out. But Helen had misjudged the setting and when the branch swooped down, it had brought the limbs of a large oak with it, sending it off-center and missing its target.

"Well, my trap failed, but we know somebody was out here."

"What if that had been somebody innocent walking through, like me?"

"Then you'd have been lucky that it failed this time."

"There's no telling how many traps like this I've breezed right past in the last three days."

"Yes," Helen said, without much concern. "The woods are full of them. It's a wonder you're still alive, lad." She eyed the top of the tree for a time, then untied the wire and wound it up loosely to fit across her chest, shoulder to waist. "Let's go, then."

Once we crossed the creek Seamus seemed to have lost the scent, so we kept to the trees as much as we could. This part of Ireland was mostly pasture and so we were completely in the open, easily seen from any hidden place along the way. I imagined a sniper's laser on my forehead where I could not see nor feel it and so I moved as much as I could, jerking my head and body to the side, moving in a zigzag, just in case anyone was aiming at us. I expected at any moment that I might see Helen felled by a silenced rifle's bullet.

Helen forged ahead as if she had no fear at all.

We trod alongside rivers and creeks that gurgled across the countryside, mostly because they were often lined with trees that offered some protection from the sight of others. Only within the trees was I able to relax a little. In one way the fear of the open spaces was better because my expectation of being murdered kept my mind off the grief that was stretching tightly across my body, pinning itself to me, weighing me down with its black mass. *My mother is dead my father is dead Arlo is dead Sera Phoebe Miriam Charlotte everyone on the boat everyone my aunts everyone everyone I ever knew all of them gone.* This ran through my head anytime I wasn't focused on the bald act of survival.

We walked an entire day barely speaking to one another yet somehow we came to know each other in that time. The only words uttered were Helen saying, "We best go this way," or I'd whisper, "Look, grapes," and Helen would reply quietly that they were gooseberries and full of vitamins before we fell back into our silence while we picked as many from the bushes as we could carry. During our quiet day I was able to better study her. Her strength. The gentle way she put her hand atop Seamus's head when we sat down to rest; they were like old friends after less than a day together. The careful but quick way she looked a gooseberry over for insects or bird shit before slipping it into her mouth, where she chewed it noisily and closed her eyes in satisfaction when one was particularly delicious. She was a person who was used to always being in motion, yet when we stopped to rest, she allowed herself to relax completely, lying flat and enjoying a patch of sunshine that fell across her face.

Around the time of sunset the world quieted and softened as it always did. I was moving along as if in a trance—
walking for hours had given me a kind of mesmerizing
rhythm. But all at once Helen thrust her hand back, palm
wide open, and turned to let me know that we should stop
and not speak. She put a finger to her mouth, her eyes on
mine and then on Seamus's, as if he, too, might understand
this sign.

Helen crouched down and took up an arm-length
branch from the forest floor, then tapped it before her, and
the ground collapsed in a fury of leaves and sticks, revealing several sharpened spikes that had been positioned in the
sinkhole.

"These woods are being watched," she whispered, and it
was clear to me that we had narrowly avoided a booby trap,
and that there were plenty more awaiting us.

We moved safely on, however, and no tragedy befell us.
Not that day, anyway.

Each time I thought back to the sharpened spikes stick-
ing out of the hole in the ground, I felt like throwing up.

Later, we made camp on the banks of a round loch that
looked like a silver mirror. A small island stood in the very
center, with a huge oak tree spreading its limbs out over
most of the ground. Helen told me that the island was man-
made thousands of years ago and there had most likely once
been a house or fortress there. Far across the water, a bird
called out in a high, lonesome song that sounded about as
sad as I felt.

"She's pining, poor lass," Helen said, her face lit silver by the reflection of the lake.

"What makes you think the bird's a girl?" I asked.

"Why shouldn't she be?"

That night we slept in shifts, but it seemed that Seamus never slept at all, as he was always on alert with either Helen or me as we looked out at the night, listening to all the live things cheeping and singing and playing their tiny instruments in the trees and grasses. I couldn't bear to look up at the smudged swath of stars because it made my grief too thick to bear.

Daytime opened, overcast and drizzly. In Ireland it seemed that there were two kinds of mornings: ones so beautiful you could hardly stand to walk through the perfect air and ones that were overcast and drizzly. And we walked. There are few miseries worse than walking for hours in a cold rain. I felt the cold all the way to my bones, and I gained blisters atop blisters from walking in my drenched shoes, which were starting to fall apart. I had tied a piece of fabric around the right one to keep the sole from flopping with each step, and while this helped to keep the shoe intact, it threw my gait off just enough to jolt my spine every time I moved. The water was in my eyes and mouth and nose and to survive it without losing my mind I had to go into a state of existing and nothing more. I was a ghost, just like those that traveled with me.

We happened upon a paved road hemmed in on either side with high hedgerows and small trees that felt like

walking through a green tunnel. We moved along in this
protected space for a few miles before Seamus stopped
abruptly and looked back with his ears alerted, his face a
picture of concern.

"Someone's coming," Helen said, looking back the same
way he faced, just as we caught the first glimpse of a truck
lumbering our way.

We clambered into the hedgerow, and a tangled bramble
pierced my chin and lower jaw with its thorns. I could not
yell out or even tend to the wounds gingerly, so I tore the
briars from my face. I kept my right hand tucked under
Seamus's collar and pulled him through with me. I had
gone to the left side of the road and Helen had gone into the
cover on the right. We hadn't had time to formulate a plan.
The truck rumbled by us, slowly enough that I could see
the two uniformed men up front, laughing together. And
then, in the back of the truck, dozens of people crammed in
together in a space only large enough for six or seven, some
of them mashed against the metal fencing that both held
them captive and kept them from falling out onto the road.
I caught sight of a few faces: some terrified, some resigned,
some simply holding on to see what came next. All of them
soaked from a morning spent in the thin drizzle. All of
them children.

I waited until the noise of the truck had gone well out
of earshot before I moved, about the same time that I heard
Helen making her way back through the brambles to get

onto the road again. I put two fingertips to the wounds on
my face and held them before me, trembling with orbs of
blood.

"If we stay on this road, I'm betting we'll find the refugee camp," Helen said. She tugged a green bandana from
her pocket and wiped roughly at my face.

"Why would we want to?" I couldn't see any reason to
go there. Everyone on my boat was dead. Perhaps Helen
had someone she was aiming to find.

"It's always best to be as informed as you can." She
folded the bandana into a neat rectangle and pushed it back
into her pocket.

"But the closer we get to a camp, the more likely that
there will be more patrols."

Helen turned the strap crisscrossing her chest so that
the rifle went from resting across her back to being easily
accessed at her hip. "Then we must be extra careful."

WE DIDN'T WALK much more than an hour before we found
the camp. Whoever had set up this operation was not very
clever or perhaps not worried about being spotted, because
they had situated it in a small valley easily viewed on two
sides from the surrounding hills, one of them speckled by
trees, the other bare. We slunk up the wooded hill and lay
on our bellies, watching. There were elevated guard towers at the four corners, with a soldier in each one, but no
patrols. The camp itself was little more than barbed wire

stretched into a large square. Hundreds of people paced or sat on the ground, staring off into space. There was no shelter of any kind. From our distance we couldn't make out their faces, but their postures were those of defeated people.

"It's a temporary camp," Helen whispered, as if reading my mind. She didn't take her eyes from the scene below. "They move them around to make it harder for the Resistance to liberate them."

"Have any of the camps been liberated?"

"Of course, lad," Helen said, as if this was the most foolish question she'd ever heard. Often her replies took on this tone of exasperation. "We need to move closer."

"Why?" I asked. She ignored me as she eased forward through the long grass by way of her elbows. But she looked back angrily when I raised my voice and said her name. "What?" she hissed.

"Why are we here?"

"Be quiet," she said sharply, turning back to look at the camp. "And either come or stay." She had said that she was alone, but I knew then that she was looking for someone, hoping to catch sight of a familiar face. She crawled on down the hill and Seamus was close behind her, keeping low. When I didn't follow right away, he glanced back as if to urge me on.

Every sound we made was heightened. Every breaking blade of grass, each scoot of knee or elbow, the swishing slides of our bellies. Even my swallows were thunderous in my own mind, easily hearable by a guard many yards away. Of course we were being nearly silent, moving with great caution, but it did not feel that way at the time. A cold sweat broke out all over my body, starting on my forehead and moving down the backs of my arms and my back. I wondered why I was following, risking myself to the exposure of those guard towers where a lazy soldier was most likely hoping for someone to approach so he might have some excitement that day. But the thought of letting Helen and Seamus out of my sight was the most terrifying thing of all.

Eventually we got close enough to see that all of the prisoners were very young. A few teenagers but mostly children. Some of the children carried smaller children on their hips. All of them had shaved heads and wore the same beige uniforms.

Helen capped her right hand over her mouth.

We lay very still for well on an hour, studying the camp. There were only the hundreds of faces to see, and they were such faces that none of us were able to look away except Seamus, who was dozing, as he was apt to do in moments of stillness.

But oh, the faces. All these years later, I can see them. They are burned into my mind.

So many of them, and their eyes were all the same. Full of the horrors they had witnessed. You may be able to see hope in someone's face, but even more clearly you can see the loss of it. Despair changes the shape of a person's mouth, the way they hold their bodies, how they look out onto the world. The eyes of the dead in a living person's face.

Most of them were sitting on the bare ground, waiting. For what, I don't know. The next time they'd be moved. Beatings. Their executions. Whatever came next. Others were milling around for no other reason than to keep moving. I knew that feeling. To move was to keep living. Even if you had to walk in circles.

After a time a pair of soldiers entered the enclosure, handing out chunks of bread that the children devoured. "Jaysus, look at this disgusting cow," one of them said. He seemed to be particularly fond of insulting the girls.

The other soldier, a boy with just the trace of a beard, held out a jug of water but wouldn't allow anyone to sup from it until they knelt at his feet. When any of them drank too fast, he gave them a kick with the side of his shoe. Somehow his quietness was more disturbing than the other one's loudness. Still, everyone surged forward when the soldiers drew near. There was no telling how long it had been since they had eaten or drunk.

I had never felt so sorry for people in my life.

And then, unbelievably, amazingly, there was a girl who looked like Charlotte.

I recalled her small hand slipping from mine as soon as we hit the water. I saw flashes of her snuggled in close to my mother. Always so quiet, a kindness always on her face.

So many times since, I had pictured her at the bottom of the Atlantic.

Was it her? The girl was dirty-faced, hair recently shaved down to the scalp so roughly that there were scabs from where the razor had nicked her. Still, I could not mistake that face. I had looked into it too many times during our crossing. I had held that small hand. I didn't know how it was possible she had made it to shore. Yet she was there. A little white moth of a girl. A barely alive girl.

Charlotte tore into the bread like a wild animal with one hand, in a decidedly unmothlike fashion. The other arm hung limp at her side, wrapped in a dirty bandage. The soldier gave her water and let it pour out over her chin and wet the front of her filthy shirt. He drew the jug away, tipped it so that a small stream ran over her head to humiliate her. Instead, she turned her face up quick enough to grab one more drink.

I surged forward before I even realized I was moving. Helen grabbed hold of my ankle, digging her nails into my skin enough for me to register the hurt. She had her mouth tightly set and shook her head. Seamus sat at full alert now and I couldn't tell whether he was ready to pounce on me to stop me from moving or if he was about to sink his teeth into Helen's hand to make her release me.

"I have to get her out of there," I whispered.

"Don't be a fecking eejit," she hissed. "We'll be murdered."

But I couldn't leave Charlotte behind. I sprang to my feet and raised the hazel stick and ran toward the barbed wire. I had no plan for what I would do, how I would fend off the two soldiers and the snipers in the guard towers. There was no courage about it, only a foolish, mindless idea that somehow I could save her this time, although I had failed her before.

Just when I reached the barbed wire fence there was a bolt of white light at the back of my head, and then:

only blackness.

SEAMUS SPRANG TO standing just as the woman did. He watched as she brought the butt of the rifle over her head and drove it into the back of the young man's head. He could hardly believe that she would betray them like this. He could feel a growl growing in the back of his throat, but then he understood.

She was saving the young man. He had run toward the danger and the only way to stop him was to knock him out. The soldiers had noticed anyway. One of them pulled his pistol and fired several shots. The older one was sprinting toward Seamus's young man, who had fallen onto the barbed wire fence. The woman was faster, though, and she ripped him from the fence. Seamus could see blood spreading on his shirt.

Now everything happened at once.

The children behind the fence rushed forward. Some of them tried to climb the fence but were tangled up on the sharp burrs. Blood bloomed in their hands as they tried to climb over.

Then the fence was down and the shots were everywhere. He jerked his head around and saw the men up there with guns causing little tufts of dirt to peck around their feet. He saw children behind the fence falling to the ground.

Seamus looked this way and that, trying to take in everything.

He saw the woman knock the gun out of the soldier's hand but just as quickly he slammed his fist into her mouth. The woman was unfazed; she drove the butt of her rifle against his nose. Seamus heard the crunch of something in the soldier's face. The younger soldier ran toward them, pushing children out of his way, and the woman drew the gun into the air and brought it down onto the soldier's head. Her face was a mask now.

Seamus sprang forward and clamped his mouth around the younger soldier's ankle until his teeth met bone. The soldier fell forward, screaming and firing his gun into the air three times around Seamus but

missing

missing

missing

until there were no more bullets. Seamus snapped his head back and forth so that the little soldier cried out more and dug his hands deep into the nape of Seamus's neck. But Seamus bit deeper until his mouth was full of blood that tasted like rich dirt and the soldier was crying and trying to crawl away.

The woman was still smashing at the skull of the older soldier. Blood ran from the corner of her mouth. He didn't quite know what to make of this woman who could be so tender one moment and so furious the next. She might turn and hit him in her fury, but he had no choice; Seamus had to get his young man away. He nudged at her leg with his nose to bring her out of her madness. When this didn't work he sank his teeth into her pant leg and pulled at her. She kicked him away, so he grabbed hold of his young man's shirt and tried to drag him up the hill but he was too heavy. The shirt ripped away from the boy's arm.

Then the woman was standing over him. Blood was splattered on her face and madness was in her eyes. She leaned over and pulled up his young man, hoisting him over her shoulder with such difficulty that she bent beneath his weight. She took careful steps up the hill and Seamus followed. Behind them there was much shooting and screaming, and he felt the sudden urge to move as quickly as he could; he wished the woman would, too. He wanted away from the terrible noises.

After a time they got over the hill and the awful sound was lost to them and there were not nips of fire at their feet anymore. He stopped to take a sup of water from a meandering creek and when he did the woman trudged right on past, not about to stop. He hurried to catch up to her and stayed close to her heels.

At the edge of a pasture, she gave out at last and fell onto her knees, releasing the young man's body onto the ground before her. She knelt there, panting.

Seamus licked at the young man's face to make sure he was all right. He sniffed down his body, trying to find wounds. There were only the small ones from the fence. The young man was breathing and moaning, clutching at the back of his head.

Please be well, Seamus thought, gulping in the scent of his young man. This is something his old man had said to him in the last days together in his delirium.

Be well

be well

be well

be.

Still the woman was gulping in air. Seamus licked at her face, tasting her sweat and the soldier's blood. Her body odor was thick. She put her hand out and sank it into the fur of his neck, then cupped his chin.

"The good auld dog," she said, struggling the words out through her desire for more air. She turned to lie on her back and latched her eyes on the sky, then on Seamus's face. "We made it," she said. "We're alive."

Seamus licked some more at her face. He wanted to tell her she had done good, the way she carried the young man.

Before long the woman rose and shook the young man by his shoulders. He moaned. "I hit him too hard," she told Seamus, and though her eyes were wet, her face was not. "I shouldn't have hit him so hard."

Then she closed her eyes and her lips moved but there was no sound and Seamus didn't know what she was on about.

Her eyes sprang open. "He needs water," she said to herself, or to Seamus. He wasn't sure which. She reached for her jug and poured a thin stream over the young man's forehead. She smoothed it there with her slender hand, then parted his lips and dribbled a bit in his mouth. "Come on, lad, come on," she whispered, occasionally looking back over her shoulder, becoming still to listen. But Seamus heard nothing behind them anymore, and neither did she.

"We have to keep moving," she said, and this time she was definitely talking to Seamus. She looked him in the eye. "They'll come for us."

She pulled the young man up to stand drowsily beside her.

"You have to walk, boyo," she said in the gentlest voice Seamus had heard her use. He was surprised she possessed such a gentle voice. "Come on, then, you can do it."

And he did, leaning on her. But he walked, never making a sound, his eyes glassy.

They went a long time in silence through a quiet wood. The trees were very large above them. Seamus could hear the trickle of a stream nearby. There were birds cooing in the trees. The air smelled sweet and green, too, the way the grass used to taste back on the island when he would go out in the mornings and chase the gulls and roll around in the pasture and chew the stems of grass. This smell reminded him of before, and of his old man, and there was a little ache in him that all of that was no more.

They walked for the longest time, and even though the young man was now able to increase his speed, still he didn't say anything. He kept rubbing at the back of his head.

When the sky dimmed and the birds quieted, the woman stopped on a rise above a river. She gathered wood and Seamus went down to the shoals to have a drink of the icy water. As he rose from lapping at the river he spied mountains rising before them. The blue haze and the round tops of the mountains gave him a moment of comfort. The sky had turned a deep rosy color and the sun was smudged behind darkening clouds.

Seamus trotted back up to their camp, where the woman had built a small fire and she and the young man were sitting close together eating in silence. She tossed a piece of the tough, spicy meat to Seamus and they sat there together, the three of them, eating and thinking of the children back at the fence.

When the young man dozed off, the woman nudged him. "Wait a bit before you sleep," she said. "That knot on your head worries me."

"You shouldn't have hit me so hard," he told her.

"You gave me no choice, though, did you?" she said, her mouth full. "You were about to get the lot of us killed."

"I wasn't thinking."

"No, you certainly weren't. And now all of those children are dead because of you."

The young man put his face into both of his hands and sobbed for a long time. Seamus sat as close to him as he could, positioning his rump on the young man's foot. The woman stared at the fire. After a long time the young man curled up on his side and pulled Seamus close to him, and Seamus rested his chin on the young man's arm. They dozed together.

In the middle of the night Seamus was awakened by the woman whispering.

"I'm sorry," she said to the young man, her voice sounding like a low purple sky.

Seamus eased away from his young man and settled against her legs where she lay. She needed comforting and if there was one thing he was good at, it was this. He knew how to be still and let his stillness make folks feel better.

"I had a son once, you see," she whispered to Seamus. "I do have a son. They took him, Seamus. So now I'm always looking for him, not knowing if he's alive or dead."

She patted the top of his head and he yawned.

"So we must never lose one another," she said. "You and me and this fella here."

Seamus gave her fingers a lick and settled himself. The night was very quiet. Before long the woman had drifted off, exhausted by everything that had happened on this terrible day.

Seamus was so tired, but now that the woman was snoring, he wanted to go back to his young man. Before he left the woman, he stood close to her face and drew in the vigorous scent of the dried blood on her mouth, then padded away. His young man was quiet and still, the way he always slept. The trees were very quiet and still, too. He knew that one of them needed to be on alert, but he couldn't keep his eyes open.

As he went to sleep, he saw his old man back on that day they had walked the whole island together, climbing to the highest point and seeing nothing but the endless, moving sea on all sides of them. He had thought back then that he and his man were the last people left alive, but he had been very wrong.

I COULDN'T STOP thinking of how sometimes during the crossing I would awake to find Charlotte curled in close to my mother, looking at me. Again I thought of her small hand being torn away from mine, her eyes on me as she thrashed in the waves. Now this, too, would be burned onto my mind's eye: the light of hope on her face when she caught sight of me as I had rushed toward the fence. My stupidity had surely killed her. I hadn't seen her shot but something in me knew she was gone. And that was too much.

I swam in a deep, dreamless sleep. When I awoke, I didn't let on so that Helen wouldn't spring into action and demand that we keep moving. I eased my eyes just wide

enough to catch a glimpse of what was going on around me.
I saw Helen and Seamus sitting nearby, watching over me.
Allowing me rest. Usually Helen's back was to me.

Seamus knew when I had paddled my way back up to
consciousness. I could feel him ease over and breathe his
hot, sour breath onto my face.

I had lain there so long that my limbs and back ached
from the stillness. I heard my parents telling me to not give
up, just as I had heard them whispering this into my ear
ever since our boat sank. But I didn't have enough life in
me anymore to stand up and do as they said. It would have
been so easy to lie there and refuse any water or food, sinking deeper into the ground until I was nothing more than a
collection of bones.

The only thing that roused me was the nose of Seamus.
On the second full day of my stillness, he put his wet nose
to my eyes. When I still didn't move, he tapped harder
and added a few small whines in the back of his throat.
I opened my eyes and he was staring at me intently. He
put his chin atop his two front paws with his rump high
in the air to show off the wide sweep of his wagging tail.
He set his eyes right on mine and whined again, then
brought his head up as if he might howl, but he didn't.
Then he grabbed hold of my wrist with his teeth—gingerly,
so as not to sink them too far into my skin—and pulled
at me.

"Stop," I told him, but the word came out more as a grunt.

Seamus dug his teeth a little deeper, causing a start of pain to run up my arm.

"Ow, dammit!" I cried out and he took a few steps back, then rushed forward again, grumbling in a way that made plain his aggravation with me. He set his eyes on mine again and when I didn't move, he ran away. I waited for him to come back and after a time I thought that he had left me. He had given up on me.

At that, I sat up and saw Helen asleep nearby. She had set up camp for us in a low-ceilinged cave. A small fire glowed between us. Seamus was sitting at the mouth of the cave, watching for me to rise. He gave the ground three thumps with his slender tail. Beyond him I could see a sky the color of wild roses, a pink that could only mean morning was breaking.

HELEN HAD CAUGHT a rabbit in one of her snares and had cooked it up with wild garlic and a couple of potatoes she had scavenged from an abandoned garden. I found half of it in a small tin she had propped on the rock ledge near the fire, presumably to keep Seamus from swallowing it whole. I didn't realize how hungry I was until I found breakfast awaiting me. I had learned that it was always best to eat meat slowly because we were so unused to having it regularly, but today I gulped it down much like Seamus might have, licked my fingers, and set to breaking camp. I couldn't bear to stay here any longer.

I knew Helen didn't sleep this soundly so the fact that she continued lying there meant she was doing exactly what I had been doing earlier—not moving to avoid having to talk to me. By the time I had everything gathered up, however, she was sitting cross-legged and stretching her arms high above her head so that a series of tiny pops sounded from her neck and back.

"I want to get going," I said. "We've been walking long enough and it's about time we made it to Glendalough."

"What do you hope to find once you get there?" she said, not unkindly, but more as if she really wanted to know.

"All I know is that's where my parents wanted to be."

Helen laid her hand across my wrist so that I stopped kicking dirt onto the fire and looked at her.

"I shouldn't have said what happened back there was your fault," she said, looking up at me. "It wasn't."

"No," I told her, "it was. Let's go."

"I killed one of those soldiers," she said, withdrawing her hand, taking her eyes from mine, looking down. "I went mad, and I bashed in his skull."

"Well, you did the world a favor." I didn't possess an ounce of pity for him. "We both saw what he was doing to those kids."

"Still, to take a life like that," she said, quietly. "It's no small thing. It's wrong."

"What about all the lives these bastards have taken?"

"I don't believe in an eye for an eye. But sure that's exactly what I did, and I'll not glorify in it."

I saw that her hands were trembling, and I should have done something to comfort her, but I didn't. Perhaps because I didn't know the right thing to do. But maybe because of a hardening that had come over me.

"I had a son. He'd be about your age now. I haven't seen him in two years."

"Where is he?"

"I don't know," she said, struggling on the words, but refusing to weep. She swallowed hard, then looked up at me again. "They took him away, to punish me."

"For what?"

"And my husband didn't go searching for food."

"What happened to him?"

"He went looking for our boy. Aidan. And they killed him."

"How do you know?"

"I found him hanging from a hazel tree in our village."

I didn't have to tell her I was sorry or comfort her. She knew.

"Why were you being punished?" I asked.

Helen looked away, the red sky offering a rosy glow to her face. "I've not told you the whole truth about me."

Seamus had grown impatient with us and now ran from the cave mouth to jump up onto my knee with his front paws and nudge me with his nose. I patted his head and when Helen began to speak again, he knew something was wrong and sat down at my feet.

"For the past months," she said, "I've been looking for Aidan. That first night, when you came to that farmhouse and found me—when you first approached, I thought you were him."

She fell silent, eyes set on her shaking hands again, and I had to look away. She was trembling all over. I wanted to tell her to go ahead and just have herself a good breakdown. But I couldn't find enough kindness in myself right then to give these words to her.

"And the worst part is that today, when I first caught sight of that older soldier—I thought that was him, too. When I killed him, it wasn't just because he had been cruel to the children. It wasn't even because I knew that given a chance, he'd shoot every one of them. I kept hitting him because he wasn't Aidan."

"I'm sorry," I told her, not knowing what else to say.

Helen stood, hunched over to avoid hitting her head on the low rock ceiling of the little cave. She stuffed her thin blanket into her knapsack, slid the rifle strap over her torso, and drew her cap down over her black curls.

Seamus was up and ready, too, running ahead of her,

then looking back to make sure we were both coming. He turned in a small circle to express his excitement.

"Let's go to Glendalough then, lad," Helen said, stepping out into the new day as if we were starting afresh.

INTO THE GREAT wide open once again.

The clear morning had been a deception—by noon the sky had gathered in gray and close, and a cold rain fell sideways, needling into our faces and down our collars in a clear effort to make us miserable. Helen and I traded shifts of walking with our heads up—one of us watching for snipers or anyone about—but Seamus kept his nose near the ground the entire way as usual. Even in a downpour he felt compelled to smell the path before him as if on the trail of something delicious.

The soles of my both my shoes had frayed by now so that water squished in with every step. I might as well have been stomping barefoot through the many puddles and mudholes on our way. When we stopped to drink from a creek I sat on the bank and wrung out my socks, knowing this would only give me a momentary relief. Seamus ran into the creek as if the water was not icy, then gave my toes a quick lick, his big eyes steady on my face.

Just then the sky let loose a ferocious downpour. Rain so big it hurt, and we had to run through the woods until we found a beech with limbs big enough to take some of the blows for us. Helen and I stood with our backs against the trunk, watching as the rain fell so hard it looked like silver curtains swaying in front of us. Lightning brightened the grayness for a moment, and then the thunder came, a monster that prowled over the hills and pastures, stomping over us, and moving on before circling back to careen about us again. Then the wind came, causing the trees around us to bow and crack, but the old beech did not waver. The sound of it all was tremendous, like bombs falling all around us, the thunder shuddering through me like the waves from sound cannons.

When the rain had died down enough that we could hear each other, Helen spoke.

"When I was growing up, storms like this didn't happen in Ireland."

I had heard my own mother say the same about back home every time the big winds and the hard rains came. I couldn't imagine a world without such storms.

Just as suddenly as it had started, it stopped. "Like a
television being turned off," Helen said, but I couldn't really
remember televisions, either.

Then: walking, walking.

Sometimes Helen sang some of her walking songs, very
quietly, and usually only a few lines from each one, as if
she could not remember an entire composition: "A Stór Mo
Chroi," "Wild Mountain Thyme," "Country Life."

"Don't you have some songs, boyo?" she asked, after
one of her songs.

I didn't know any of them all the way through, but I
sang the verses and choruses of all the songs we used to
sing back on the Preserve: "Angel from Montgomery," "No
Hard Feelings," "You Got Gold," "The Story."

Helen laughed and clapped when I had finished. "That's
gas! I've not heard those songs in donkey's years."

For long stretches there was only the sound of our own
footsteps.

As we walked there was not much to see: the back of
Helen's green jacket, turned greener by being soaked
through; the slick leaves of trees; the tiny yellow flowers
and big thorns on the gorse in great clumps all along our
way; little Seamus jogging along as if he was perfectly
happy to trudge across an entire country—always glancing back at me. But most of all there was the white haze
of rain between us and the wide pastures, between us and
the round-topped mountains to the east. There could have

been a dozen soldiers or the Banished or any manner of evil all around us within a few feet before we would have been able to see them.

Other times we talked of nothing to entertain ourselves.

"Today what I crave the most are ninety-nines," Helen said as we talked about foods that we missed.

"Never heard of those."

"So unfortunate you are, then," she said. "A vanilla ice-cream cone, with a chocolate flake. Janey Mac, it was delicious! We always had them at the seaside, and sometimes I would get one for Aidan out of the Applegreen petrol station if he was on good behavior when we drove into Cork City."

"I miss peanut butter," I offered.

"That's dull of ye," Helen said. "I was expecting you to name a McDonald's cheeseburger or the like."

"All of that kind of stuff closed down when I was still too little to remember."

Seamus had been trotting along happily beside me but now he raced ahead of us, drawn by some irresistible scent.

"You're better off in a way, lad. Hard to miss what you never had," she said. "We had a few more years of normalcy than your country, so Aidan had longer to experience all of that."

"What I miss most is just being with my family."

She had been trying to lighten the mood and now I had dimmed it once again. I felt bad as soon as I said it, knowing the grief she carried as well.

"Aye, I know all about that," she said, then added after a moment: "And now you have me craving peanut butter, too. I used to spoon it straight from the jar."

We neared Seamus, where he was enjoying a fine time of rolling around on the wet ground. I was sure it was something nasty—the remnants of a dead animal or perhaps a scattering of fox manure. As soon as I came close, he bolted to his feet and went back to jogging alongside me. He'd not be sleeping anywhere near me tonight unless the rain washed him good and clean.

Suddenly the rain started again—large drops that fell in misty sheets like swaying curtains in front of us—drumming the leaves and the ground with such ferocity we could no longer talk. We fell into silence and as always, my mind wandered to the past—my parents, the sweet-smelling woods of Maine, the bruised-blue Atlantic.

Arlo. Taking hold of his hand. Bringing his knuckles to my mouth. A kiss against them. His cedar scent.

All those ghosts, always right at my heels. When my parents had told me to always keep going, they had not only meant with my legs, but with my mind as well. Perhaps keeping the mind moving was more important than the body anyway. At first Glendalough had been my destination just because that was where they had told me to go. But now I began to think about how I might be aiming for it just to possess a destination. I had been on the move for so long now that I could not even imagine sitting still once I got there, the way we had back on the Bigelow Preserve during those days when everything had seemed perfect for me even though our country was burning down all around us.

"—so let's check it out." I realized I had only caught the tail end of something Helen had been saying to me, but her finger was pointing to a white house that was coming into being out of the mist ahead.

I never liked the idea of checking out houses, even though I knew Helen was right to always be on the lookout for any supplies. Still, I feared stepping into a house containing corpses. I had seen plenty of dead bodies in my time but there was something worse about being in an enclosed place with them, especially one that might hold anything around any corner. Even worse would be to happen upon living people in their own homes.

As we neared the house, I saw that it had less promise of holding anybody inside, though, since the front door was completely off its hinges and several windows had been busted—or shot—out. A pair of yellow curtains stirred in one of the windows. Someone had used orange spray-paint to write on the wall next to the front door:

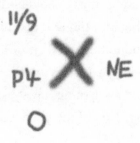

A small rusty car sat pulled up to the porch with its hood, trunk lid, and driver's door standing open. A raspberry bramble had completely overtaken one end of the house, as if swallowing it before our eyes. To one side a metal gate stood open, revealing a barnyard populated by farm implements in various states of decomposition in front of a red barn with a caved-in roof.

We approached carefully, easing up along the hedgerow and watching for any sign of life. Just as we stepped out into the yard, there was the zip of a drone overhead. The sound of it was unmistakable, the sound of something trying its best to be silent and only just failing. Yet we could not see it. Helen hoisted the rifle up onto her shoulder, pointing it skyward as she scanned the tops of the trees.

Seamus's ears went on alert, and he stood with one leg curled in toward his chest, his eyes looking to the pasture beyond, and back to me as if I might be able to confirm for him that I heard it, too. A small whine escaped his throat.

We waited, crouching down there for a long time, but we did not hear anything again. The drone must not have caught sight of us.

Helen told me and Seamus to hold back, and she hurried into the house. Although I thought the rain might be about to lift, I could see pounding curtains of it shifting through the mist over the wide pasture as another cloudburst came toward us. I watched everything, my eyes scanning all that was within my sight. Part of me knew that there was little use in doing this. At any moment soldiers or the Banished might come barreling across the field toward us, prepared for slaughter.

Before long Helen came back out with what she had found: a single can of sardines that had been missed by earlier scavengers. She grabbed hold of the latch and pulled back the top of the tin, producing a bloom of salty air and the little fish in a bed of olive oil. We divided them up— six each—and I sucked five of them down in one handful, pausing to let them linger on my tongue for one second so I'd remember having eaten something. I held my hand out with the sixth sardine lying on my palm and Seamus gingerly sucked it away from my fingers and wagged his tail, shaking his rump around, wanting more.

"Anything interesting in the house?" I asked.

"Shots had been fired in there," she answered around her last sardine.

"How do you know?"

"Bullet holes in the walls." She wiped her mouth on her coat sleeve. "Bloodstains on the floor."

"Recent?"

"Oh, no," she said. "A year ago, at least."

She tipped the can up and let golden olive oil slide into her mouth, then handed it to me so I could do the same. The oil was the most delicious thing I'd tasted in ages: the taste of Spanish hills I'd never see, Mediterranean Sea air that I'd never smell. I felt the energy to walk throughout the night if need be. And the rain had stopped as if a switch had been flicked to turn it off.

"And look here," Helen said. She pulled a small metal canteen from one of her jacket pockets and tossed it to me. "Found this."

A treasure. Now I'd be able to carry my own water.

Helen put her hand into another pocket of her coat. "But boyo I have saved the very best for last. That house was a goldmine." She withdrew a pair of red socks from her pocket and held them out on her palm to me.

"I can't take them," I said, desperate to take them. "You found them, you should have them."

"I'm too much of a selfish cow to offer them to you without having gotten a pair for myself," she said, and pulled up one of her pantlegs to show a new pair. Hers were purple.

I could have wept from the joy of such a treasure and sat down to put them on. They felt so good to my ravaged feet that they might have been made of silk instead of rough wool.

"Well, no sense in dawdling," Helen said, and began walking before I could even begin to hustle the pack onto my back.

Onward, then. For miles and hours. Into the purpling of evening. "The gloaming," Helen announced, and I wondered how the world had known in all this time to start its way toward nighttime without Helen around to speak it into being.

"Why do you call it that?" I asked her back. She was balancing herself with her arms out as we crossed a jagged line of stones across a quickening stream.

"What would you have me say instead?"

"Dusk. Twilight," I answered, watching the cliffs above us. I was always more nervous around rushing water like this because it limited what we could hear of the rest of the world.

"But the word *gloaming* is so much lovelier," she said, as if that was that, the end.

Tall pines loomed all around us, fragrant with sweetness, and then we came out into a clearing where we could see the silhouette of mountains against the darkening sky. The mountains lounged against one another in various states of repose.

"I should think we're two days' walk from Glendalough," Helen said, more to herself than me, as was her custom.

Several starlings arose from an ash tree atop the wooded hill before us. At least a hundred fluttered skyward. They all moved together, as if they could predict each other's movement. They swooped down, and up, and in a spiral movement. An undulation. Dozens of birds moving as if they were of one mind. I had seen this happen before, but it always felt like a kind of magic.

"A murmuration," Helen breathed out.

"That's a good word, too. Did you make that up?"

"No," Helen said. "I collect good words."

"Where do you find them?"

"Everywhere." After a moment, she added: "I was a teacher. In a gaelscoil."

"What's that?"

"A school where you're only to speak Irish. Before the Britons took over again."

"Why didn't you tell me that you used to be a teacher?"

"You never asked," she said with an air of annoyance. "What were you? Before you were a refugee?"

I had always felt so at home in the Maine woods that I had never even thought about how we had really been refugees there, too, hiding out. "Ever since I've been a child we've just been trying to survive."

By now we had reached the large ash tree and the birds had spun away in one rippling mass over the far pastures, where the last light was leaving the western sky. We stopped there, beneath the ash, where two hazel trees grew beneath it.

"What is *murmuration* in Irish?" I asked.

"'Ealta,'" she said, then took hold of one of the slender limbs that had grown up in a bramble around the older, thicker branches of the hazel. "And this is 'coll.'"

The tree had shed a limb that was the perfect size for a walking stick. I had missed my hazel wand ever since losing it at the camp, and I took this one. Helen had set her fists on her hips, scanning the level ground around us. I knew what she was about to say before she suggested we set up camp. She always liked to rest on a high point where we had the vantage point of looking down on the land.

The sardines had been delicious, but already I was famished. The five little fish were all I had eaten the entire last day. We had only a few dried mushrooms left—chewy-crunchy in their staleness—and a couple handfuls of plantains and dandelion greens we had gathered along the way. I wanted more fish, more olive oil. I wanted rabbit or squirrel or quail—the thought of the greasy brown meat made my mouth water. I wanted peanut butter. I wanted to try a ninety-nine. I think we ate in silence that night because we were both so dissatisfied with our suppers. I wondered if she was imagining all the delicious things she had ever eaten, just as I was. When I lay down to sleep while she kept watch, I had an awful time dozing off despite my exhaustion, because the growling of all three of our stomachs kept nudging me awake.

Until finally: rest.

AT FIRST I thought the foxes had come back to study me in my deep sleep, but it was Helen, her voice so quiet and close to my face that it was little more than warm breath. My eyes fluttered open to see her leaning down so close that our eyelashes nearly touched. Behind her, an eerie lavender sky.

"Somebody is here," she whispered again, and this time I heard her so clearly that I started to bolt straight up, but she had anticipated this and already had my shoulders pinned down. "Stay still."

Down by my leg I could feel the warm presence of Seamus, and most of all I could feel the quiet-engine-like hum that growled within him when he was on alert.

I heard a branch break in the woods. Not too close, but close enough to hear. The rustle of leaves. We knew the sounds of the night well. We knew every sound you could hear outside, and these were definitely the sounds of a person, or of people. Then, the sound a person makes when they are trying to be silent, more like a disturbance in the air than a noise.

A long silence.

And then, another cracking branch, such a startling snap that Helen and I both jumped up at the same time. She already had her rifle out and up in front of her before I had even wrapped my fingers around the hazel stick. Seamus had sprung into action, too, trembling with rage toward the sounds, his teeth bared, although he refused to allow any sound to escape. I knew what I'd have to do if someone came out of those woods, and I was ready. I gripped the stick tighter. There is an animal in all of us who knows how to survive.

We stood there, in the blue hour, those most silent moments of the night an hour or so before the sun would show itself. The darkness was still there but lightened, and even though there were dim shadows, somehow I could see everything better than in full daylight: the lines of the trees, the angles of the hills, the shapes of leaves, all of them more distinct.

Another branch cracked, but this time, farther away. Whoever was near was leaving. Daylight was coming into being.

We were already traveling by the time day had tightened the corners of the sky with its whiteness. We had not gone very far before we smelled the acrid scent of something burning. Woodsmoke, for sure, but more than that. A sweet, dull smell beneath the woodsmoke. The farther we walked, the more intense the aroma became. Once we made our way over several hills and through two glowing green valleys, we could see the northern sky was heavy with smoke that first appeared to be a thin gray, then a dark gray, then a near blackness overtaking the horizon there.

"That's not Glendalough, is it?" I asked, almost afraid to put this into words, as I knew that the settlement lay in that direction.

"No, I don't believe so." Helen watched the sky, and I could see the worry on her face, even if she would not give voice to it.

I was relieved; if she had said yes, I think I might have sat down right there and given up. There would be no use in anything if the only place I had to aim toward was reduced to ashes. Glendalough had become more than a word my parents had said over and over. Glendalough had become my parents.

I was about to ask her if she had been through this territory before when we came up a small rise and Helen put her hand out behind her and then turned her face enough to show me that she had a finger to her lips.

And there they were, right in front of us.

＊ ＊ ＊

THE MAN WAS hanging upside down from a catapult trap, swinging by one ankle bound by a thin, strong rope that was cutting into the meat and bone of his leg, causing blood to bloom there. The mess had run down the insides of his legs, collected at the waist of his pants, staining them a shining burgundy, then crept down his chest to drip from his nasty chin.

He was dead. He hung there like an L—one leg straight up, caught in the snare, and the other straight out at a ninety-degree angle, since it was free. He looked as if he had been beaten nearly to death. One of his arms hung at such an angle that it had to be broken. The closer I looked at his face, the more it seemed to me that his mouth wasn't setting quite right, as if his jaw had been knocked completely askew. His head was several feet from the ground and the girl was standing beside him with a hunting knife drawn. The girl who had saved me and Seamus days before. The man who had taken ahold of my neck. The tracker.

The girl looked to be out of her mind. She gripped the knife before her and stared up at the hanging man, and just as we approached, I could hear her say: "Da." The closer we got, the more easily I could see that he was certainly gone from this world. I couldn't tell if she was about to cut him down—by shimmying up the tree to slice the rope—or if she was going to draw an X across his face. "Da. Da. Da," she said, pausing for two heartbeats between each utterance. "Da. Da. Da." She did not even realize we were standing a few feet away. The longer I looked at her, though, the more I believed that she didn't know which she wanted to do, either—desecrate him or save him. She looked the way I had felt when I had that passing thought that the death of the baby on the *Covenant* would at least bring us some peace and quiet: a mix of relief and guilt.

"Drop that knife," Helen's voice cracked the still air. Her rifle was aimed directly at the girl's head.

The girl looked at the knife then back to us and then she threw it down.

"What are you doing?" Helen asked, and before the girl had time to reply she shouted: "Tell me. Now!"

"The trap caught him," she said, her accent much thicker than Helen's. "And I didn't know what to do."

"Were you about to cut him?"

"No," she said, as if she were refusing a piece of bread.

"He's dead, lass," Helen said.

The girl looked up at him and recoiled, as if she had not looked at his face before this moment. She wore a necklace outfitted with several silver medallions, as if she had collected them over a long period of time.

"Were you his prisoner?" Helen asked.

"He's my father."

"As if that answers my question." Helen was moving toward her now. "Roll up your sleeves."

The tracker's body turned so that he was no longer facing us, and I believed I could hear the wire cutting into his leg.

"Hurry!" Helen lunged the end of the rifle at the girl. "Roll them up now. Show me!"

The girl unlatched the button on her right sleeve and pushed the sleeve up to reveal a tattoo in small, haphazard print spelling out RONAN.

"The tattoo on your face isn't enough for ye, is it? So you're called Ronan, aye?"

Ronan nodded, casting her face down.

"Why did you look at her arms?"

Helen ignored me. She wound duct tape round and round the girl's thin wrists, binding them, then squatted onto one knee and patted down Ronan with her free hand, checking for more weapons. There were none, so she worked fast at binding the girl's ankles together.

She held Ronan's hunting knife out to me behind her back so I would take it. Just as I stepped forward, Ronan flinched. At my heels, Seamus whined, which was unlike him in such a situation.

"Please don't kill me," Ronan said, more a statement than a plea, to Helen instead of me as I took the knife. "Not like this. I'll do whatever you want."

"Nobody's about to kill you," Helen said. "We're not animals like you lot."

"I *know* who you are," the girl said, her voice rising with each word. Her face was a scowl of terror. "*What* you are."

Helen drew back her hand and brought the sharpness of her open palm to strike the girl's face. "Shut up," Helen spat just as their skin connected. The crack made me startle. She thrust herself forward, her own mouth inches from the girl's. "Shut your filthy fecking mouth right now or I'll shut it for you!" Helen stepped back and brought her rifle up again. "Do you hear me?" she said, and the girl nodded her head. "Who beat him like this?"

Ronan gave a deer's stare to her, likely to convey that Helen had just told her to be silent.

"Answer me!"

"The trap popped him up in the air and slammed him against the trees."

Helen looked up at the tracker, his wild rat's nest of black hair hanging straight down. His body twisted back around and revealed his face to us again. There was not as much soot there as the first time I had seen him so I could easily make out the B tattoo on the right of his face. His stench washed over me as the body turned again in the light breeze and I had to put my hand over my mouth to keep from gagging. His body was so disgusting in every way, and I flashed back to his wild eyes as his strong hand had clenched my throat. Yet still he was a human being, like me, like Helen, like all of us. Mean and ugly and stinking, but a person nonetheless.

"Good enough for him," Helen said, a new kind of anger shaping her face, "to be left here hanging like a slab of meat."

"No," Ronan said. "He's my father."

"I had a father once, too, and a damn lot of good he did for me," Helen said, then turned to me. "We need to tie her up. Now."

"Why?" I kept seeing that moment she had saved me and Seamus in the woods play out in my mind.

"The tattoo on her face tells you why. She's been banished, for betraying the Resistance." She turned to face the girl. "You can stay here with your disgusting father and cut him down yourself once we're long gone."

"Please don't leave me," Ronan said, her words small and even, carefully spoken so as not to sound as if she were begging us. "Not out here alone."

"And take you with us so I have to watch you every second of the day?" Helen let loose a sarcastic laugh as she peered into her knapsack. "Not likely."

"I know what you did!" Ronan screamed, muscles rising up in her neck. "You're the—" Suddenly Helen had plucked the gray roll of tape from her knapsack and wound it round and round Ronan's head, but before she could, the girl got out two more words: "Black Fox!"

The girl was screaming now with little success behind the thick tape, but Helen was completely focused on completing her task, her mouth tight like she might be about to bite. Now she held the girl against a young beech and wound the tape around her torso and the trunk of the tree so she couldn't move.

"What are you doing?" I was speaking to a wild animal. In her eyes was the look a bear might have as it stomps through the forest. She had told me she didn't believe in an eye for an eye, but these two had apparently made her forget all of that.

"I'm securing her to this tree. Then we're going to Glendalough, just like we planned."

I couldn't leave the girl there to watch her father's body as birds plucked the skin and muscles from his bones. He didn't deserve to be cut down: he would have killed both me and Seamus that day if he could have, and there was no telling what he had done to his own daughter. There was no sense in spending any time on climbing a tree to cut him down and to bury him. But I had to intervene for Ronan's sake.

"We can't just leave her here like this. It's cruel."

Helen stopped taping long enough to turn and face me. "I'm only securing her well enough to give us plenty of time for a head start. In a few hours her wild ass will have gotten free of this. She knows how to survive out here. Don't let her innocent act fool you."

"But still, to leave her here alone," I pleaded, "with no weapons—that's wrong."

Helen's shoulders relaxed and her face softened, rounded. "I was ready to just lie down until you came along. But I wanted to help you get to Glendalough. You reminded me of my son, so I got up."

"I don't know what any of that is supposed to tell me."

"That means let's not let this rubbish slow us down. Don't you know what people like this complete arsehole and this girl did to my son and husband? It's *their* fault—"

Behind us the girl was saying something, over and over, more and more loudly. "Mow. Her. Mower. Mudder." Her eyes were boring into Helen and even behind the tape and her inability to move her lips the word was clear: *Murder. Murderer.*

Helen drew back her hand and slapped the girl across the face. "You lot were the murderers!" Helen yelled.

Tears sprung to Ronan's green eyes, but just as quickly she thrashed and pulled away from the tree with her shoulders, not fazed by the duct tape. Helen was standing over her, taking great breaths, and I feared she might strike the girl again, but she didn't. "You lot," she said again, under her breath now.

I eased forward and got as close to her as I dared. "Helen," I whispered, "please. Enough."

She stared down at Ronan. After a time she turned and walked to the creek. She bent down, cupped her hands into the water, and splashed her face. I went to her.

"What did she mean by calling you a black fox? What murder is she talking about?"

Helen stared at the ground, clenching her jaw. Then she set her eyes right on mine.

"I led a band of the Resistance for a time—" She paused and was quiet for so long that I thought she might not say more, but just when I was about to prompt her, she continued. "We planted landmines in the roads we knew only the Nays traveled. We sabotaged their vehicles and hid bombs. This whole area was rife with camps. One for children, like the one you and I saw. Another for the white immigrants, one for the people of color. We tried to help them all. For selfish reasons, too, though. I was looking for my son in each camp. But more and more of my friends were killed, and then it was just me. For the past few months, I've done what I can to fight them on my own. For Aidan."

"Aidan," I said, just to say his name aloud, but she misunderstood and thought I didn't know who she meant.

"My son," she said, her eyes flicking to mine just for the brief second it took to utter the two small words. Then away again, as if she couldn't bear to look at me. "At some of the camps I just snuck food to the fences. In the night I'd pass bits of bread and slices of orchard apples through the holes in the wall to them." Helen paused, slid her knapsack off, and set it on the ground beside her as she sat on a fallen elm. Seamus went to her immediately and she put out her hand. He rested his snout on her palm, and she petted him while she talked. "But then, at one of the Slieve Séipéal camps, I messed up. This was a camp where they kept the sick and elderly who had hidden rather than turn themselves over to be shipped off to the cities. Some of them had wished only to die in their own homes, in their own Ireland. A couple of them were from my village. They had all been brought there to the Nays by traitors, some who later became the Banished. Some of whom were never found out. Bounties. They made money hunting the sick and elderly. Despicable." She nearly spat the last word. Helen's hands were trembling in front of her. She slid them under the sides of her thighs. "I made too much noise leaving the fence and they searched everyone, found the potatoes and soda bread I had brought that night. Beat those who had the food. Tortured them out in the middle of the camp for everyone to see. Castrated one of the men and let him bleed to death."

She had been studying the woods around us, but then she looked up at me. "Sit down," she said. "I don't want you hovering up above me like that."

I took a seat beside her on the fallen tree.

"None of them would describe me or say my name. Each of them claimed to have never seen me. So they lined them up and shot them, one by one, in front of the whole camp. The oldest must have been in her early eighties."

Helen leaned down and kissed Seamus atop the head. I had never seen her be so affectionate with him before. "Each one, they'd demand a description. And when they didn't reveal anything, they were murdered. All of them could describe me but they wouldn't do that. Some of them knew my name. Yet only one of them revealed that I was called Helen McPartlan. Only one told them what I looked like. But they killed all forty nine of them."

Behind Helen, Ronan struggled against the tape around her shoulders and wrists, kicking at the ground with her bound feet, making no progress at all. She was pitiful to watch but maybe if she wore herself out now Helen would be less resistant to taking her with us.

"The Nays took the corpses to the church at Slieve Séipéal, scattered them around the grounds and inside the building, and spread the word that I had killed them. Said that I was a member of the Resistance who killed them for being Nays loyalists, which they were not, of course. This was back when there were still enough people around those parts to matter, to be a threat to them. They wanted to get a mob stirred up so they'd find me, but their plan backfired. Most of the people didn't believe it. They knew the real story. And they started calling me the Black Fox. Slinking around in the dark. More called me a hero than a murderer. But I wasn't either one."

Helen took a moment. Shook her head. "I was just a woman grieving the loss of her son and her husband by carrying food to people imprisoned for being themselves.

Fighting back any way I could." She conjured anger back up into her throat. "That little bitch knows the Nays killed all those people, but she hopes to put doubt in your mind about me. For all I know those two were bounty hunters for my own head. Things like her can't be trusted. Because the Banished have left their humanity behind. They're the opposite of you, lad."

"But to leave her to die out here—I don't want that on my conscience. We'll take her prisoner. We'll keep her bound the whole time. But we can't leave her."

Helen sat looking at the ground. She shook her head, then cocked her head to set her eyes on mine.

"Very well then, but she will be your responsibility. She'll have to remain tied to you for the whole journey," she said. "Once we get to Glendalough we'll turn her in to the Resistance and they can suss out what to do with her."

I stood. "Why did you want to see her arms?"

"They mark themselves with tattoos for every bounty they take in," she said. "Like a badge of accomplishment for every life they destroy."

"But she had no marks for that."

Helen looked at me without expression. "Not yet."

BEFORE WE LEFT we had to search the dead man's body to see if there was anything of value. He was hanging just high enough that most of his body was out of reach. There was no other choice except for me to get on all fours and let Helen stand on my back. This was easier than climbing the tree to cut him down. Helen was light and balanced herself with ease, so the worst part was staying in that position. She narrated as she went along, telling me that she had found a metal slingshot shoved down into the back of his pants and a small coil of metal wire—probably for strangulation—attached to one of his belt loops, which she easily popped free.

"Ah, sure he has brass knuckles in his other pocket," she

said. "Hold on a little longer. I'm going to pat him down." She found a knife strapped to his thigh and jabbed the tip of her own knife into the fabric enough to rip open the pant leg. "Oh, Janey Mac, what an odor!" she called out, about to gag. She unlatched the leather holster from his leg and hopped down from my back.

As he turned again I could see eight marks on his right forearm. Eight acts of treason against his own people.

I sliced through the tape at Ronan's ankles and she held forth her arms so I could do the same at her wrists, her large eyes steady on my face as I slid the blade back and forth.

"If you try to defy us I'll kill you without losing a wink of sleep," Helen said just as the last thread of tape came free. "Do you hear me?"

Ronan nodded.

I put away my knife and brought my fingers up to the girl's face to peel away the tape Helen had sloppily wrapped around her head. Ronan's eyes widened as she looked into mine.

"You don't need to be afraid of me," I whispered. "I remember what you did for me."

"What are you doing?" Helen hollered. "She doesn't need to speak to walk."

I took off the tape anyway. There was no sense in it. "There's no harm in removing it," I told Helen, but not without a quaver in my voice. I did not want to defy her but

I also couldn't stand how pitiful Ronan looked. She was so small, somehow even smaller now, as if humiliation had deflated her. Her wrists so thin, her hunger so obvious.

The peeling away of the tape left Ronan's skin red and splotched. Her mouth was trembling when I eased the tape away from it, and I could see small jagged rectangles of her lip's skin standing on the tape. Tiny dots of blood bloomed on her lips like needle pricks.

"It's. Over." These two words seeped from her like three breaths—one long and two short. I could only reckon that she was talking about whatever she had gone through with her father.

HELEN AND I foraged as we walked that evening but our supper was meager: water celery—too swampy to produce even the hint of a crunch—with a salad of bitter hogweed seasoned only with a fistful of cow parsley.

I couldn't much blame Ronan when she refused to eat. I had tied her to a tree a short distance from our place by the fire and she had lain down with her back to us. I wanted to tell Helen that I had seen her before. I couldn't fathom Ronan's own reasons for having not said anything about it so far. But still, I kept quiet.

Helen and I had always talked in the evenings by the fire but that night we sat mostly in silence, watching the flames and smoke. Seamus settled as close to my leg as he could get, as he so often did, but occasionally he rose and sauntered over to sniff at Ronan. Each time when she didn't acknowledge him, he stood looking at her, flopped his tail a couple times, then came back to settle in beside me.

After awhile the girl fell asleep there on the dirt. Helen said she would take first watch, so I positioned my pack behind my head and put my arm around Seamus there beside me. A little humming snore reverberated in his chest and he moved closer, stirred, brought his nose down to press wetly against my fingers. They say it is foolish to put human qualities to a dog, but I couldn't help feeling like he was loving me, and I was reminded of how long it had been since anyone had touched me in a caring way. All of my life, there had only been four people to really do that: my parents, Sera, and Arlo. And now this good old quiet dog, maybe one of the last ones. He had been alone in the world, just like me. Dogs had always been taken away from their mothers and siblings early on and had to create their own families. Whoever was good to them became their family. I searched with my fingers until I found his big, silky ear and held on to it until sleep found me.

OVER THE NEXT two days, we walked through an ashen forest. For miles everything had been burned. The few trees that were left were black skeletons against a low, gray sky. The green meadows had been turned into black char that crunched beneath our feet like frozen snow. We passed through a village where buildings had been burned down to their foundations. When I protested that we had to turn back, that there'd be nothing to eat in this wasteland, Helen kept walking, the muscle in her jaw tightening.

"We're going to Glendalough," she said, low, walking on.

"But it will be burned, too," I said.

"Glendalough will never be destroyed," she said, and hastened her step. Once she had told me she was only going along with me to Glendalough because she no longer wanted to walk in circles. Now determination rested on her shoulders. "They've done this only to keep us away from it."

I could only assume that the *they* she spoke of were those who were anchored in at Glendalough. I couldn't imagine a more foolish defense—destroying all the plant life for miles to preserve your own patch of it—but this was Helen's country, after all. She knew more than I did on most counts, and certainly about Irish doings.

For half a day I was nauseated. I thought this charcoal scent would rest in the back of my throat and I'd never be rid of it. Even now, all these years later, just thinking about those days of misery conjures the smell and makes it wash up over my face. Even Seamus took on a sneezing spell that lasted most of the day, trying to rid the scent from his nostrils. He didn't help matters by insisting on drawing in great nosefuls of the ashes as he trotted along. While Helen and I could occasionally cap our hands over our noses and mouths, Seamus and Ronan could not. Seamus for obvious reasons but Ronan because Helen insisted that her hands remain bound behind her back. At first Ronan made no complaints about this. She had been led across the country on a leash bound to her father's wrist for who knows how long, so this was most likely tame in comparison.

"She's marching us right into the belly of the beast," Ronan whispered to me in a moment when Helen had gotten far ahead of us on the path. It was late in the evening and the dimness of night was gathering. "She's taking us to the Nays. She'll sell us."

"You don't know what you're talking about."

"She's the Black Fox." Her voice was hard, but when I turned to look at her, fear covered her face.

"She's not what you think," I said, realizing that by whispering back to her I was somehow participating in a betrayal.

"But maybe she's not what *you* think," Ronan said. "You might be her prisoner without even knowing it. The Black Fox is patient. She combs the countryside, looking for stragglers, and they pay her well when she brings in her bounty."

"I *know* her," I said, but I cannot help admitting that a violet of doubt opened in me. In those days it did not pay to trust anyone completely. I could hear myself speaking and knew that I must have sounded to Ronan as if I was trying to convince myself more than her.

"Why did you help us, that day?" I finally said.

"It was for the dog, not you. I couldn't stand to see my father do that."

This made sense to me. "I hope he didn't punish you too much for it."

"He wasn't always like that. The world turned him into a monster."

"Why did he have you on a leash? That seems pretty monstrous to me."

"This from the man who has me on a leash right now," she said, bringing her bound wrists up before her.

"That's different. We don't know if we can trust you or not. He was your *father*."

"Well, he never sold me. That's what this feckin' bitch intends to do."

"She's not like that."

"I know you think she's your friend but she's a bounty hunter, Lark."

Something about her saying my name broke her momentary spell on me, and I saw again that she was back to her original goal of converting me into an ally. I would not abide someone manipulating me. I told her to shut up, now, and she did. As if she had heard me, Helen stopped at the top of a little hill a few yards in front of us and turned to me. "I can see Blessington Lake."

"What's that mean?"

"That means we're close to Glendalough," Helen answered. "And up ahead the burned land stops."

WE CREPT OUR way along the small paved road with high hedgerows on either side of us after having spent two whole days in a world devoid of any colors other than black and gray. My sense of smell seemed heightened now that I could draw in the scents of leaves and grass. Occasionally old beech trees loomed overhead, big and stout as ancient columns. As night settled, I could see the slouched shoulders of dark mountains in the distance. On either side of us were green fields—a glowing green that revealed how close we were to the lake—pocked with the charred corpses of cattle that Helen said had been put down when all of them had become diseased.

And then we came down to the lake, the largest body of water I had seen since leaving the ocean. A bridge carried our road across to the other side, but before crossing we stopped to look at a beach where small waves lapped. Seamus padded down to get a drink. The lake was calm and quiet: the opposite of the threatening ocean I had barely survived.

"Please, can I rinse off?" Ronan asked.

Helen was beside me, working at the intricate knot I had learned on the *Covenant* as she tried to untie the rope from my arm.

"What are you doing?"

"She needs to bathe," Helen said. "Go on ahead of us. Wait up on the bridge if you like."

"Now?"

"Yes, *now*," she said, her impatience escalating. "Jaysus Mary and Joseph, will you untie this mess?"

I couldn't help but wonder if she was going to do something. Execute this girl, perhaps. "What are you up to?"

"I'm up to nothing more than allowing her to clean herself." Helen held my gaze as if I shouldn't say more, but then she realized I was too dense. "It's her time of month, you eejit."

I untied the knot and called for Seamus. He followed me up to the bridge, glancing back a couple times to make sure that Helen and Ronan were all right. Tank-sized rectangles of cut rock had been set at the ends of the bridge to block any vehicles from going over it, but these were easy enough to squeeze between as people on foot. We sat on the highway with our backs to the concrete barriers of the bridge. I looked up and saw that several stars were shining above. Lyra. Vega. Libra. A gibbous moon revealed its whitish-blue surface.

I glanced down to the beach to make sure that Helen had told me the truth about allowing Ronan to bathe. Helen sat on the bank with the rifle across her legs, looking across the lake as Ronan waded out with the water striking her mid-belly. Helen had tied the rope to a large tree near the water's edge and had released Ronan's hands from the restraints so she could wash herself. Apparently Helen had allowed her to borrow her precious cake of lavender soap because there were white suds on the water. Ronan opened her blouse to wash and I looked away. Only then did I realize how much Ronan reminded me of Sera. They didn't look alike so much but there was something about the way they moved, something about the fierceness that was barely contained beneath their skin.

After a time, Helen marched up the bridge with Ronan trailing behind, a rope running from Helen's hand to a loop around Ronan's waist. None of us spoke as we crossed the bridge and moved into the thick woods. It seemed that no one had been in this place for years. Brush threatened to overtake the road. Houses that sat close to the pavement were being devoured by the wild, walls and chimneys and garages being eaten so slowly by the woods that their movement was not visible to the naked eye but was undeniable all the same.

WE CAME TO a small stone church that stood very close to the road, like most all of the buildings in this village. ST. JOSEPH'S CHURCH, a sign announced, 1803. Out front a tall Celtic cross had been knocked down. It lay in two intricately carved pieces at the foot of the cross's base. One of the heavy wooden doors stood halfway open. Helen pulled out her gun and held it before her as she stuck her head in. I followed close behind, the hazel stick pulled back and ready. Ronan crept so close to me that I stepped back onto her foot a couple of times. Inside, the church was black-dark until our eyes adjusted enough to see nothing more than several wooden pews that had all been pushed into one corner. The altar had been pummeled with a sledgehammer, too, which meant that the Nays had been through here at some point.

We all homed in on it at the same time, a flash of brown and white galumphing toward us. The smell of the old cow—damp and shit and musk—washed over us. The cow knocked Ronan down and her weight pulled me onto the floor. The cow's back hoof came down hard on my leg, causing jolts of light to register behind my eyes in one painful second, and then I could hear its hooves gaining traction and speed on the stone floor as it exited the church, Seamus close behind.

I jumped to my feet, amazed that my leg wasn't crushed, but I felt hardly any pain as I ran out to catch the cow. Ronan was still attached to me and at first her slowness jerked me back, but I gave the rope a sharp pull and she followed along, telling me to slow down, but I ignored her. The old cow lumbered weak with hunger and had spent all of its energy rushing toward the door to make its escape, so by the time she reached the road, the pavement seemed to defeat her. She crumpled very slowly, her front legs going out from under her as if she were kneeling down like the stories of Old Christmas my mother had told me, when the animals would fall to their knees and talk aloud throughout the night. I drove my knife into her neck until the jugular had been sliced to make sure she did not linger, and the old thing went completely still after a few seconds. There was no thrashing of hooves. Who knows how it had survived as long as it had out here. My hunger was larger than my sorrow for the poor animal. I knew the meat would be stringy,

but it would be meat nonetheless. I had had only the greasy
leg of a rabbit since long before crossing the wide ocean and
my mouth watered at the prospect.

You do not know what hunger can do to you until you
are hungry, so don't go thinking I am heartless.

WE FEASTED AFTER roasting steaks over the fire. It had
taken me two hours to butcher the cow despite its meager
offerings, and I lay down that night exhausted yet fuller
than I had felt since I had left Maine.

We slept in the church that night although something
about it made me uneasy. I would not know what until
daylight. I slept fitfully, awakening several times to find
Helen sitting in one of the wooden pews with her eyes
on the door. Once I could have sworn that her head was
bowed in prayer, but she sat erect when she felt my eyes
on her. Helen had a sixth sense for that kind of thing, a
heightened sense that almost always kept her a step ahead
of me.

Ronan's rope offered us both a good three feet of pri-
vacy, but I didn't trust her enough to allow her to sleep
near, so I had tied her to a heavy pew. She slept as silently
and as unmoving as the dead. At least twice when I awoke,
I found that Seamus had wedged his rump against my legs,
his two front paws paddling softly as he dreamt of chasing
rabbits or squirrels or whatever he might have chased in
his life before me. Just as the sky edged into a deep pink

through one of the broken windows, I dreamt of a constant creaking. But when I came fully awake, I realized that this sound was true. I could hear it, just outside the church walls, the sound of a creaking rope.

I took over my guard shift and allowed Helen to sleep. I spent the entire hour watching as dozens of chips of colored light collected on the middle of the church floor. The colors came from a high window where a Christ outfitted in several shades of purple was reaching into his chest and revealing his crowned heart. A trio of doves fluttered in through one of the windows and sat in the X-shaped wooden trusses, cooing while they studied us.

The lighter the day became, the louder the creaking became. When morning had completely taken over the world, I went outside, following the sound out the back door, which opened into a stone courtyard where another large cross had stood before someone had knocked it down and turned it to rubble. Just beyond it was a raised bed that held four heads of cabbage and several dark green shoots of onions. I pulled up the onions and then I saw the bright orange nubs of carrots just underneath the wet soil. I pulled up one of the carrots, wiping away the dirt and eating the entire thing in three quick chomps. I now recognized potato plants, too, and I scooped underneath them to reveal five small potatoes. I loaded up the bottom of my shirt with this bounty and when I turned back to face the church, I saw the source of the creaking.

An entire family—two adults and two children—hung by their necks from ropes tied to the highest points on the church. Who knows why or by whom. Those were misery days that defied justice or explanation. They had been there long enough that I could only tell their ages by their sizes, so whatever monsters had done it were long gone, but I still wanted the hell out of there immediately.

I rushed back in. "We need to go, *now*," I said.

"Cabbage!" Helen cried out, then she looked up to my face. "What did you see?"

"A sign that we're not supposed to be here."

Helen snatched up her knapsack. She gave a sharp tug to the rope tied around Ronan's waist. "Come on, lass," she said. But Ronan would not rise.

"Just leave me here," she said, sleepy-eyed.

"We're not leaving you here alone," I said.

"It'd be better than being turned over to the Nays," she said to me, then turned her gaze to Helen. "You know what they'll do to me."

"I'm not going to turn you over to anyone. We'll get to Glendalough and the group there can decide what to do with you."

"Just go," Ronan said. "Please."

"It's not safe here."

"I've survived worse places than this," she said. "I'm sick of being your prisoner."

"Too bad," Helen said, and gave the rope such a jerk

that Ronan was forced to scramble to her feet. "I don't trust you enough to leave you here to track behind us."

I didn't know what to think any more. Perhaps Helen did intend to sell the girl. Maybe she was afraid Ronan would follow us and ambush us when our guard was down. Or perhaps she felt the need to protect her but was too stubborn to admit as much.

※ ※ ※

BEFORE TOO LONG we were engulfed by the Wicklow Mountains, which rose at a steady pace and reminded me of being back in Maine. If only I had known then what holy years those were, on the Preserve in Maine. We never realize the halcyon days until they are over. Now that I am old, I can look back at my long journey across the Atlantic and then Ireland, both the tragedy and beauty, but at the time I lingered on the misery. Mostly that time was nights of freezing and starving, of never-ending terror. Days of blistered feet and weary legs, of constant hunger. The only thing that carried me through was an occasional surprise of beauty among all of the desolation: the startling yellow of gorse, the glowing green of mossy rocks in rushing streams, the gray skies, the churning sea, the crumbling stone walls. The trees, the trees. But most of all there was the way the little dog walked alongside me. The fierce set of Helen's shoulders.

Ronan was having a harder time navigating this terrain with her hands bound. I asked Helen to take the restraints off after Ronan had fallen a couple times as we climbed a steep rock, but she refused to allow it.

"You don't know what these things are capable of," Helen said. "They're animals, Lark."

The third time Ronan fell, she hit a large tree root face-first, slicing open her skin just above her right cheekbone and along her eyebrow. She had fallen just shy of a high drop that would have sent her plummeting and that would have pulled me over with her. Blood ran down into her eyes and she couldn't wipe it away.

Everything hit me at once: I couldn't catch my breath and the world was spinning around me. I could feel my heart beating and a cold sweat covered my back instantly, causing me to shiver uncontrollably. I sank to the ground, leaning my back against a tree.

All the dead swam around me. Not just those I loved, but every corpse I had walked by, every human being I had seen shot or beaten to death. All the animals who had died and suffered. All those who fought against it. All those who stood by while it happened. Most all of them were dead now and what did any of it matter, anyway?

I felt a wetness at the tips of my fingers, the simultaneous softness and roughness of the dog's tongue, licking me back

into consciousness. I looked down and Seamus looked up
at me.

I plucked the knife from my belt, and as I held it before me
Ronan recoiled, begging for me to not kill her, and her face
was my mother's. Sera's. Charlotte's. I slid the knife through
the rope that bound us together. I could hear Helen yelling
no, could sense her running toward me. But I cut through
the ties at Ronan's hands anyway, and she gasped—in relief
or shock. A second. Two seconds. Then she looked up at me
with a face transformed. No longer pitiful. Instead, wiping
the blood and dirt from her face, she grabbed the knife away
from me in one swift motion and drove it into the side of
Helen's arm down to the bone. Helen let out a shattering
scream and crumbled to the ground on her knees.

I tried to stand, but the world was still spinning and
I hit the ground again just as Ronan wrenched the knife
from Helen's muscle and held it in both hands over her
head. She pulled the knife back and then Seamus ran at her,
teeth bared and a growl low in his throat. For the first time
since I had known him, he barked, a rapid fire of barking,
a bark that had been waiting for so long to be set free. He
advanced on her as if he might sink his teeth into her leg,
but she kicked at him as she backed up, tripping over a tree
root and falling hard to the ground, dropping the knife. She
kicked out again and landed such a solid blow to his head
that Seamus fell to his side with a weak yelp.

I grabbed the knife and ran toward her. But she knew

what was about to happen. She could feel the pull of it at her back. She had stepped out on the sharp edge of a small cliff that loomed over a fifty-foot drop, and I still cannot be sure if she gave herself to the air or if gravity took her. I will never forget that split second of relief that was etched onto her face as she fell backward, sailing through the sky until she landed, her spine crunching across a fallen tree.

I BURIED HER myself. And I do not blame her for what she did.

It took me a long time to come to that realization, though. Back then I didn't know hardly anything. I am ninety years old, and I still don't know a whole lot. But I do know that the worst thing in this world is the intolerance that leads to so much violence. I have had to put it on the page to draw our attention to it so we would be disgusted by it.

The only thing I knew for sure that day was that many circumstances—mostly the actions of those in power—had led to that moment and a million others just like it. Everyone who benefited from devastating the natural world. Everyone who participated in the misinformation and discrimination that led to my country's collapse. Everyone who gained power or money from war. Ronan's death was a complete waste of someone who could have possibly lived much longer and better. I had never seen the girl so much as smile, but she was a human being and because of that, I like to think that she had the possibility of joy within her.

I didn't grieve when I buried her. And I don't recall feeling angry at her either. I just kept thinking what a tremendous waste all of it was, all of the people who had died because of the few who had benefited from burning our world down around us. I've heard people say, "We destroyed our world," but I don't agree with that. Some of us did. The rest of us were powerless. The rest of us are the ones who had to pay the biggest price.

I buried her deep. Deeper than necessary. I couldn't stop digging. I put all of my anger into digging that grave, so much that I fear I might have cursed that ground. I have happened by that spot a few times over the last seventy years, and it is a barren place now. A circle of dirt in a cluster of bushy yew trees whose nettles won't even collect there. A lonesome place. I did not wish that for Ronan. I simply buried her where she fell. I put a stone there a few years back, with a large *R* carved into it.

I HAVE GOTTEN ahead of myself, as it would be a week before I went back and buried her.

As soon as Ronan fell over the cliff, I turned to find both Helen and Seamus behind me. Helen had managed to prop herself against a tree where she sat clutching her arm, her face going from a bluish gray to a frightening white unlike I had ever seen before. She was struggling to keep her eyes open, looking up into the treetops as if something there held her entranced. Not far from her was Seamus, who was lying where he had fallen, on his side. One of his back legs was pinned beneath his body but the other one trembled, occasionally jutting into the air with a burst of energy or pain. His eyes were open and searching for me as if he could not move his head, and he was whining quietly.

Perhaps it is wrong of me, but I went to Seamus first. I had to choose between them in that moment and perhaps he seemed worse off to me. Or perhaps I trusted him more.

I ran my hand over his nose, and he stared up at me. Three louder whines escaped his throat now. I felt down his back and around his stomach. I'm not sure what I thought I might find—a broken bone, perhaps, or an area that was so particularly tender he would cry out to let me know the problem was there. I felt nothing out of the ordinary, but for him to lie still like that meant that something was very wrong. Internal bleeding, maybe, from the vicious kicks she had given to his ribs and head.

"Oh, buddy," I heard myself say in a quivery voice, and my tears dropped onto him. I could take a lot, but I didn't believe I could take losing him. Not here, like this. Not before we got to Glendalough.

I looked to Helen and saw that she had gone limp, slumped against the tree now, and I thought she had died.

"Helen?" I took hold of her hand, covered in the blood running down her arm, but felt no response there. "Please, Helen."

I was going to lose them both. I was going to be completely alone in this devastated country, in a world teetering on the edge of the end.

She worked her mouth in such a way that I understood she needed water, and I uncapped my canteen and poured some over her lips and chin. I capped both hands over the blood rushing from her arm, pressing down hard, and she let out a jagged scream and brought her hand up—weakly—to strike me before she realized that I was helping her. I took my hands away only long enough to dig into her knapsack and find her scarf, which I wound round and round her arm tightly.

Seamus had risen to his front legs and was scooting himself toward us, dragging his back legs behind him and yelping with each movement. I told him to stop, yelling out "No!" so sternly that he stopped. I caught hold of one of his silky ears between my thumb and forefinger, massaging it to give him some kind of comfort.

I felt torn between the two of them, trying to keep them still and calm while I also tried to figure out what I might do. I considered running the few remaining miles to Glendalough to find help, but I couldn't leave them here like this, unable to defend themselves.

We had been through too much. We had fought as hard as we could. We had walked across the country with bleeding feet, with very little in our bellies. Misery days. I had a terrible thought, one that no one should ever have: that we might all three just sit there and die together. The problem was, it would take me much longer to do so since I was uninjured.

"We have to walk," I told Helen. "We're almost to Glendalough."

"I can't," she slurred, as if she were dreaming. "Let me sleep."

keep going keep going keep

"We're so close now. We can't stop."

"Leave me," she said. "I just want to rest."

"Helen—"

"If I can be still for just a little while then I'll be a . . ." I felt her hand on my forearm and looked down to find her clutching my shirtsleeve between her fingers, her hands cut and scabbed, her fingers lined with black dirt.

I checked the scarf and found that the bleeding had been quelled for now. Helen was a bluish pale and breathing in quick, short breaths. I tucked my hand into Seamus's armpit and could feel his heartbeat galloping along just as it always did, which I took as a good sign. I wasn't sure what was the right thing to do, but if I let them rest for a short time, we might have a better chance of making it to Glendalough.

"Just long enough for me to make supper," I said. "Then we're walking."

Helen laid her head back against the tree again, startling at the pain in her arm before letting rest cover her up. I put my face down to Seamus's, eye to eye, forehead to forehead. There was no use saying anything to him. I didn't need to. He knew what I was thinking just as I could read his mind in that moment. I would not let either of them die. I wouldn't leave either of them behind. I'd make supper and get them to Glendalough and then, at long last, I could rest, too.

I ROASTED THE pitiful potatoes, carrots, and onions over a fire that I kept well stoked, constantly placing more wood on it as I kept watch over Helen and Seamus. Both slept, both looking so peaceful that one might have guessed not a thing was wrong with them. I could hardly allow myself to think what might happen. Helen could lose her arm, or worse. Seamus could die from whatever Ronan had done to his insides. To keep from thinking, I worked. I gathered more wood, cupped my hands to blow on the fire, turned the vegetables, wetted a rag to put to Helen's forehead, then squeezed out a few drops onto Seamus's muzzle since he refused to drink.

The night sounds came as the earth turned its Irish face toward sunset. We certainly would not be making it to Glendalough before dark. I listened to the sound of the fire, watched the comfort of its flames and sparks, feeling like I ought to savor it all, somehow. Feeling like it all might be about to end. I had no idea that I stood on the hinge of my life that night, that by tomorrow everything would be completely different.

I roused Helen long enough to feed her bites of the potatoes and carrots, blowing them cool before putting them to her lips. She ate them the way a person does when they are not hungry but know they must take sustenance. Seamus turned his face away when I tried to get him to eat. I could offer him nothing except petting. Last, I gave Helen the onions.

"Chew them slowly and hold them to the roof of your mouth," I told her, for my mother had taught me of their restorative power. We sat together in silence for a brief time, and she swallowed them with some effort, closing her eyes against their slickness in her throat.

"My son is dead," she said. Tears formed in each eye and slid down her face but were not followed by any others. "I know he is. I've known all this time, but I thought if I said it aloud, or quit looking, that would make it true."

"I'm sorry, Helen," I told her.

"He was so beautiful and good. Not just because he was my own, either. He truly was."

"I'm so sorry," I said, and I was. So sorry I could feel it. "I never should have trusted Ronan."

"You're the only person I've trusted since I've been on my own," she said. "I think it's simply because I chose to.

On the night you arrived at that house, I was so low that I had to. And I reckon I chose wisely."

"I was so stupid," I said.

"Don't go trusting everyone, Lark. But if we can't trust a few people in this world, then there's no point at all," she said. "It's one of the things that gets us through."

"I lost my true love. Arlo." I hadn't said his name out loud in a long time. Helen brought her arm out from behind the coat I had spread over her so she could take hold of my hand. I felt a pang of guilt at betraying my mother; I had promised her I would never tell anyone. But she had thought I would never be safe if I did. "And my best friend, Sera. Their mother, too, all three at once during our journey to the refugee boat."

"There's not a one among the working people who don't have similar stories," Helen said, "so we ought not be feeling sorry for ourselves. But sometimes it hurts so bad it feels like a knife turning in our guts, doesn't it?"

I didn't have to respond. I had to take my hand away from hers to cover my face. I stood, wiping my eyes with the backs of my hands. The grief was always so close, always waiting. One thought could pull it all back to the surface, causing me to feel like I couldn't catch my breath, causing my heart to pound. Helen must have felt the same way.

There was no more to say. I knew that the best thing for all of us was to be still and quiet. She sat there looking at the crackling glow of the fire until she drifted down into sleep. I lay down beside Seamus and put my nose very near his. He didn't like being breathed on like that, so he moved his snout away, but only a little, so he could look at me. When a dog looks at you like that you can read his mind and he can read yours.

I SLEPT VERY little and got everything assembled long before daylight.

I helped Helen up, and she had trouble finding her balance but after a moment she shooed me away. She said she could walk on her own, although she agreed to take my hazel stick to lean on. I clicked my tongue to see if Seamus would rise and follow me and when he didn't, I scooped him up and carried him in my arms. He let out one solid yelp and then a nervous whine but settled after I petted him and cooed to him for a bit. He was a gangly old boy but a skinny one from all of the walking and having very little to eat. He seemed light at first but very heavy after a while of climbing the mountain. I put my face down into the nap at the back of his neck where his patches of black, white, and tan met. I drew in his scent, which somehow always managed to smell musky and clean.

HIS MAN CARRIED him.

There was nothing but him and his man.

WE FOLLOWED THE trail down into a valley that widened out with high ridges on either side of us, barren smudges in the bluest part of nighttime. Helen leaned most of her weight on me as she trudged along, so weak she could barely walk, and Seamus accordioned out across my arms. A river crashed down the mountainside, curving alongside the trail and rushing over huge boulders in such a cacophony that we could hear nothing else. I had come to very much rely on my hearing to make me feel safer. Our ears did us no good at all in this loud place; anyone could have been coming toward us on either side of us and we would have known no difference.

Twice Helen had to sit down on the river's edge and splash water onto her face, trying to not let on to me that the pain was shuddering through her in waves. I didn't say anything when I saw that the scarf binding her arm was soaked with blood again.

Seamus grew heavier in my arms, not just because of distance but because he seemed to be relaxing against me more and more, growing into a dead weight that I didn't want to think about. I clutched my hand to his chest to reassure myself that his heart was still thrumming along and it was, but he certainly had no strength.

Please, please, please is all I could think, asking the stars or the river or the trees or whatever might listen to help him. I thought Ronan must have broken his back or given him such a lump in his head that he was forever addled. At this thought I hated her and was relieved that she was dead. It was wrong of me, but I could not help it. I said, "Please please please" to Seamus, but he gave no sign that he had heard me. I put my lips to the top of his head.

The heavier he became, the more I clung to him. If he was not in my arms, I'd not be able to keep going. I felt his weight was propelling us forward, attached to the ley lines in the place just down the twisting river from us, on a ridge overlooking the two lakes where Saint Kevin had once prayed for seven years.

I eased Helen onto a boulder and squatted down beside the river where I held Seamus's face close to the water. He would not drink. I splashed some onto his snout in the hopes that it might slide into his mouth, but he did nothing more than ease open his eyes, then fade away again. There was nothing else that could be done.

As we went on Helen became weaker, and now the full weight of her body leaned against mine. That, along with the heft of Seamus in my arms, made me move as if wading through mud. I had been walking for days now, with very little sleep in between, and with fear riding constant on my shoulders. My body had never been wearier. I had taken plenty to drink at the river but I was immediately parched again. I was too tired to maneuver across the jagged rocks along the river's edge. I was cotton-mouthed and my legs felt so heavy I wasn't sure I could lift them much more. My arms were suffering a strange mixture of pain and numbness from Seamus's weight, which seemed to increase with each step.

When I was little and sick, my mother used to sing a song to me. An old song by a band she loved. I could hear her sing the same line over and over, so clearly. I could hear her perfectly in my mind and I hummed along. I was unable to sing, but I could hear the words. I could hum to keep myself awake.

This one goes out to the one I love

And I thought then, we could have our people with us anytime we wanted, in our minds. It was not having them physically that was the harder part. Right then, I had Seamus in my arms and Helen resting against me. We were a pitiful trio, stumbling down that rocky path.

We didn't hear the guards who descended upon us like blackbirds, guns and knives drawn. They came into being out of the trees and hillsides, out of the river's edge, only shouting at us when they were near. I was so exhausted that I could barely make out their faces. Even death would have been a relief at that point. I could feel them pulling Helen away. I heard her cry out. Only when they tried to wrench Seamus out of my arms did I begin to fight back.

HELEN WAS WHISPERING my name, but I had difficulty pry-
ing open my eyes. Then I startled awake all at once, rising
up and slapping at the ground to lay a hand on my walking
stick. I found an actual bed beneath me, fashioned of wood
splits, and a thin mattress that had been stuffed with something soft. I could not understand where I was. There were
four walls, one of them with a closed door in its middle.
Across from me Helen was sitting on the edge of a similar
cot. Something looked different about her face. There was
a light there I had not seen before.

"Have they taken us prisoner?"

"No," she said, almost a laugh more than a word.
"They've taken us *in*."

I remembered the guards taking hold of us in the inky dark. Plucking Seamus from my arms.

A jolt of dread ran through me. "Where is he?" I hollered out, but then I saw him resting on a pallet on the floor beside me. He looked up at me, moving nothing but his eye, then he eased back into sleep. I jumped from the bed and leaned over him, running my hands over his head. In that instant of not knowing where he was, I had been sure he was dead.

"You were delusional from no sleep," Helen said. Her arm had been tightly bandaged with a white cloth and rested in a sling that was knotted at the top of her shoulder. "They gave you valerian root and knocked you out. I've never seen you sleep so long."

I remembered, but as if I was recalling a dream. Flashes and starts. A man tending to Helen's wound. "Drink it," a hateful woman telling me, holding out the tea. My hand on Seamus's head as sleep found me, like a dark figure swooping down to cover me with its cape.

Seamus flopped his tail only once, then went back to sleep.

"He'll be all right," Helen said, sounding more reassuring than certain. "Sure he's a strong auld man."

A woman with eyes the color of thunderclouds eased open the door. She had a huge pile of auburn hair, pulled back to show her wide, clever forehead. She was the kind of person who looks friendly even in her refusal to smile, a kind of quizzical and pleased look on her face. There was a hardness, there, too, a sign that she would be good to anyone who deserved it but strike down anyone who crossed her. A small stuffed bird hung from a brown string around her neck, the bird's green iridescence catching the light. I had not seen anyone wear any kind of jewelry in so long that I was puzzled by why she'd be decorated in such a way.

"How are ye?" the woman said, the three words running together in an upward curve.

"Lark, this is Johanna. We knew each other in the Resistance."

"Thank you," I said, wanting to say more, but I was not able to wrap my tongue around the right words. So I repeated myself. Still Johanna did not smile, although a kindness gathered around her eyes in response.

"Let's get you two fed," she said.

I ran my hand all the way down Seamus's back, lightly, for fear of hurting him. His eyes fluttered but did not open this time.

Our little cabin stood near a large communal space surrounding a fire that was sending sparks into the cool morning air. Thick beams of sunlight fell through the overstory. Children played near the fire. Three women sat watching over them while infants fed at two of the women's breasts. Not far away two young men, about the age of myself and Arlo, were sitting with their shoulders touching, talking quietly to each other as if no one else were around. Then I saw that their hands were clasped. There was an open-sided hut where half a dozen people prepared breakfast. Two elegant chestnut horses were tied to beech trees a few yards away. They took turns stamping their feet lightly when I looked at them, as if saying hello.

Once people became aware that we had awakened and stepped out of the cabin, a low murmur roamed through the crowd and people gathered close, gazing on us as if we were something to see. I didn't understand until I heard some speak it: "The Black Fox." A young woman stepped out and thanked Helen for her service, which made Helen blush and drop her head.

"You liberated the camp where my brother had been taken," the woman said. Her lip was trembling. "You saved him."

Helen said nothing. More of them were surging forward, but Johanna put one hand on my shoulder and the other to the small of Helen's back and steered us toward the open kitchen where the food had been laid out. There was a large bowl full of blueberries, as well as toasted bread and jam. A round cake of yellow butter, which I hadn't tasted since I was a child. So there were cows somewhere here, too, then.

We took a hunk of bread and slathered it with jam and butter, cupped a handful of blueberries, and sat at the long tables and ate together. I caught myself gorging on the berries and tearing into the bread, gulping it all down at once. Then I saw how the others were taking their time with their meals. Helen had her eyes firmly fastened on her food, however, and was scarfing it down like a bear might, grunting in satisfaction without realizing it. I elbowed her and she gave me a sharp look until I nodded to the others. She looked up, realizing how wild we seemed in comparison, but went right back to it.

Now I took a bite gingerly and closed my eyes to savor the butter, slick on my tongue, so delicious that a start ran down my back. I had not eaten at a table since leaving Maine. I had not sat upon a bench. I certainly had not slept on a bed. There was too much to take in at once, but more than anything there was the murmur of voices around us. People at ease with one another in a large group. I had not seen this happen since I was a small child, and it filled me with both joy and suspicion. The feeling of being within a community made me think on how wonderful people could be, sometimes. But I also knew how terrible they could be. I focused on the tart jam to re-center my optimism.

THERE WERE ABOUT forty of them at Glendalough. These were pioneer people. They came from all over Ireland, but mostly the south and the west. Two of them had made it out of Scotland before the collapse, the last remnants of a packed boat that had been sunk halfway across the Irish Sea. Many of them had family members trapped in the walled cities of Cork or Dublin. Three had journeyed all the way from Africa. One from the Mediterranean. Most of

them were orphaned people, like me. They had all fought
their way here, many experiencing worse horrors than anything we had encountered. In the days to come many of
them shared their stories with us, whether they had escaped
refugee camps, the walled cities, or by riding rafts across
the Irish Sea. Yet their survival had enlivened them instead
of killing something inside them. Or perhaps Glendalough
had restitched them somehow. It is hard to say if a place
makes people a particular way or if the kind of people who
congregate there shape the place. Either way, there was no
malice there in those days. That would come much later.
There is always someone who must rise to power, after all.
But in that first week we were there I sensed nothing of
the kind, and of course we were welcomed with such open
arms because I was traveling with the famous and beloved
Black Fox.

They had organized a settlement up on the mountain
where they could look down on the original monastic settlement, which was now a tall stone tower that had once been
used to watch for intruders, surrounded by several crumbling churches and an ancient cemetery. Farther away stood
the ruins of a resort hotel and a visitor's center, both now
burned to the ground. Below us were also the two lakes in
the narrow green valley that gave the place its name. The
mountain was alive with raucous birdsong and enormous
ferns, massive boulders covered in moss that sometimes
glowed. The way the light shimmered there. The way the

air felt. There was something about the place that I cannot name. A feeling of comfort, of time stretching itself out.

"People have been praying here for twelve hundred years," Helen told me. "Even if you don't believe in anything, there's something to be said for that."

Not all of them believed that Glendalough was a thin place, but some of them preached the power of the ley lines as if it were gospel. They had been unharmed—unapproached, even—for nearly a year there. Better to not question it too much.

"The place was nearly destroyed seven hundred years ago by the English, so we know there's no magical force field," Johanna told me. We had walked up to St. Kevin's cell together. This was the beehive hut where the old monk had supposedly lived alone and prayed for seven years. I remembered how the first night I met Helen, she had told me about the Seamus Heaney poem, the abbot praying so long with his arms outstretched that a blackbird had built a nest in his open palm.

Johanna sat down on a wide, flat rock. "But if there's good to come out of all of this collapse, perhaps it's that we can have mysterious things in the world again, yet still believe in science. I don't want an explanation for everything. Do you?"

I didn't answer her at first. I looked down at the breeze worrying the surface of the upper loch. I watched as this wind busied the leaves of the hazel, ash, and rowan trees between the water and then eased up to smooth over our faces and pass on. She didn't seem to mind my silence, and when I turned to face her, she had closed her eyes, drawing in the scent of the water, moss, rocks, and trees.

"My parents would have agreed with that notion," I said. "They'd be so glad to know I made it here."

"I'm glad, too," Johanna told me. "But to be honest it's mostly because I've pined for Helen ever since I first knew her. She's remarkable. So I'm happy the pair of you found your way to us."

"Me too," I said, but even as I said it, I felt a nudge that all was not right and that I was not speaking the truth.

WE HAD BEEN there for nearly a week when Johanna told me Seamus couldn't stay.

They had nursed him and Helen both. Helen would not lose her arm and before long she'd be able to use it just fine. They all tried to wait on her hand and foot despite her protests; she would have none of it and lost her patience easily when anyone mentioned her sacrifices for the cause. "You should let them give back to you," Johanna chided her. "It's selfish of you to not allow them that. They feel like they owe you." But Helen knit her brows and walked away.

Seamus had broken ribs and internal bleeding from Ronan's kicking, but he had survived, and he would do well, too, they told me. That first week, except for meals, I rarely left him. Once, when I had dozed off beside him,

I awoke to find that he had risen before I could stop him, grimacing and yelping when his ribs gathered in pain.

He had been lying curled up at Helen's feet. She was propped against a large pillow as if in deep sleep, but she opened her eyes after I had him settled again.

"You saved us," she said. "You could have left us behind."

"No, I couldn't have," I said, and that was that.

When Johanna came, I was sitting on the floor with Seamus in a rectangle of sunshine that fell through the small window of the hut, studying his legs spotted with tannish brown. Now that they were healing he had tried to get up a few times, but the pain in his ribs soon sat him back down.

Neither Johanna nor Helen said anything for a time. They sat there with me, looking down at Seamus.

"We didn't think a dog was left in Ireland," Johanna said after a while, leaning in close. "They've been gone a long time here."

"I know. Back home, too," I said.

"And with good reason, Lark. We barely have enough food to feed ourselves. And they don't do any labor the way the horses do. It's a terrible thing, but that's the way of survival these days, and you know it as well—"

"What are you saying? That he's not welcome here?"

"I'm afraid so, lad. It was decided when we first settled here. We can only afford to have animals that work. Seamus can't even be a guard dog."

"Having babies was outlawed, too, but that didn't stop you all."

"That's different," she said.

"If he can't stay then I won't stay," I told her.

"They've helped him get better, but he'll have to go back into the woods. He's obviously a smart lad," Johanna said. "He'll make it on his own."

"If he goes, I go with him."

"Yes, Johanna, we thank you for all of your kindnesses," Helen said, "but we can't stay without the auld man."

Johanna nodded. "I understand, but I hate the thought of you being on your own. The group won't want that either. But if we start changing the rules for one person, then we have to—"

"You don't owe us an explanation," Helen said.

Johanna ignored her. "We're good people here, Lark. But we're survivors."

I imagined going far beyond their boundary, perhaps back to Blessington Lake, and leaving Seamus there. I saw myself demanding that he not follow me, riding away on one of their horses so he'd be unable to keep up, looking back to see him standing there, still as a tree, watching me go. The thought made a thick grief wash over me. There was no way.

"We survived on our own all that time," I said. I must have sounded like a defiant child. "We can keep on doing that. We'll make our own settlement."

"You'll have to go back out beyond the burning line."

The thought of having to go that far back out into the dark country was daunting, but I didn't let on. I gave a firm nod.

Johanna put her hand on the crook of my arm. "Lark, he's a dog—"

I pulled away from her grasp. "You don't understand. He saved me. I can't abandon him. I won't."

"It's the only way," she told me, and I knew that she believed what she was saying. If you have not gone through something like what the little dog and I had been through together, you cannot fathom it.

I could not look at her.

"We want you all to feel free to stay another week, to rest and heal." Now she patted Helen atop her hand. "All right?"

Helen nodded.

"And if you change your mind in that time, you two are welcome to stay here as long as you want. From now on."

"Thank you," Helen said, "but that's never going to be."

Johanna waited for some acknowledgment from me. I was not about to offer any. I was disgusted with anyone who would want to turn out Seamus, even as I understood their reasoning. She folded her thin, long fingers together and kept a serene look on her face that made me want to scream. Then she slipped out the door and eased it shut behind her.

WE HAD A week of eating their venison and vegetables. Nights of people playing music and telling stories the way we used to do back in Maine. Everyone loved on Seamus all of the time. They marveled at having a dog about. The younger ones had never seen a dog in their lives, of course. And some of the older ones teared up when they petted him, recalling their own dogs. They certainly didn't seem like people who wanted him to be cast out, so I knew that it was only the powers that be who had made that decision.

There was a comfort in dozens of people gathered together. But I had grown used to the easy silence that had existed between myself, Helen, and Seamus. I felt suffocated by community even while I longed for it. Going back out into the wilderness would not be so bad at all if not for the threat of drones and the camps and starvation, none of which were small considerations. Seamus bolted to attention one night as if he'd heard a menace barreling through the woods, even though none of us could hear a thing. After that he was able to walk again, albeit with a limp at first. But after a couple of days even that was gone and there was the promise of once again zooming through the woods and pastures with him. That was all that I cared about.

Here is the part I will ask you to be patient and try to understand. The thing is that Helen and the dog and I could not have stayed even if they had relented. We had become

wild people, you see. Helen and Seamus and me. Not fit
for society. We were people of the hazel trees and cedars,
of cold creeks and wide pastures. We were the trout that
swim in the darkest reaches where no one can betray us.
We had more in common with rocks and rivers than we
did with people now. We had seen what happened when
people lived together in too big a clump. The better choice
was to live with a handful. There is strength in numbers but
there is danger in it, as well. Danger of one desiring a rise
to power. Danger of many being blinded by one and doing
his bidding.

But they did relent, in a way. Johanna came to us and
said too many of them wanted to protect the Black Fox.
Too many of them had grown used to having the dog about.
So, a compromise was struck.

They asked us to build our own places on the other side
of the lakes, near the Poulanass Waterfall, whose music has
accompanied my life ever since and will be in my ears as I
die.

Apart from them, but not completely. We would not eat
with them during their communal meals. We would fend for
ourselves and also help to protect them. We would be the
guards on that side of the settlement. Far enough away to
be our own people yet near enough to be of use to them if
needed. We had some doubts about being so close, but once
we climbed that mountain, we accepted it without discus-
sion. The oak trees stood like columns all around us, the

understory busy with hazel and holly whose branches were often full of redstarts and wagtails. Great spotted woodpeckers swooped overhead the way drones used to. This was a wild patch of land in a thin place. Maybe a thin place can be conjured by people praying for thousands of years. This one had been created by birds cooing in the morning mist, by the soft spray of a waterfall, by the way the light filtered through the glowing leaves. There are all kinds of beauty in this hard world and if you ask me, none of them can be matched by wildness.

We built two small cabins from the sturdy ash trees. One for me and Seamus and another for Helen. We went to the settlement on the mountain every once in a while, and always Seamus was greeted as if he were the King of Ireland, with folks kneeling down to pet him, to marvel at him licking their palms and looking them in the eye. Sometimes we went weeks without seeing anyone and that was just fine by us.

We were a homeless people who made a home with each other the best way we could. As thankful as I was for Ireland, I never stopped pining for my own country, even though I knew it was gone.

The world rebuilt itself in patches, but it is still small. Factions rose and fell. The weather increased in its fury. Shorelines and cities crumbled into the oceans. The fires died away and crops were sown in the ashes. By the time we received news it was usually months or sometimes years old.

Even when the rebels had their victory and Ireland began its reconstruction, we remained at Glendalough. People creep closer these days, though, talking about us wild people who don't have any desire for things to go back to their idea of normal. *The world is too much with us*, my father used to say, quoting Wordsworth. But we will never return to the way it was Before.

I am living here still. Who knows how much longer, because I'm not able to rise any more. I am old and white-haired in a way I could have never imagined myself. I am an apple, rotting from the inside out. Some days I still feel like that young man who walked from the southwestern coast of Ireland to the Wicklow Mountains. Some days I awake and think that if I could get out of this bed, I could do the whole journey all over again. But then I think that I would not want to do that without Helen and Seamus.

I've burned, and that's what I wish for all of you. To burn with anger, desire, joy, sorrow. All of it.

There have been other people in my life. But they are not part of this story. A person does not have one life, but many, all within the same lifetime. No matter how many years and people that came and went between, I never got over Seamus and Helen. I could always hear my parents whispering to me. I could remember Phoebe playing her fiddle in the gloaming. And I've never loved anyone the way I loved Arlo. All these years later, I still dream of him. I wake up feeling happy and sad at the same time. As soon as I open my eyes, I am overjoyed that I had time with him again, but then a freshened grief washes over me when I realize he is still gone.

For the most part, after we reached Glendalough, our story was a happy one, because we were together. There were days of hunger and misery that lay ahead for us. There were days of starting all over. We did not give up. We lived. Days of celebration and mourning. Times of quiet and fire, of low storm clouds and skies so blue they stirred up that ache of melancholy that comes with witnessing beauty. Days of simply surviving. But always, there were days of wonder.

I've been through many hardships, just like all of us, but most days the grief is balanced out by the pleasures: a delicious meal, the smell of cedar on my hands, the sound of rushing water, good friends. Joy and sorrow are the things of life, the two things always tangled together. Anybody who's ever lost anyone knows that.

THIS SEEMS LIKE a good place to hush. To be still.

Seems to me that I've told what is important. You already know what happened to Helen and Seamus, eventually. We live, and then we die.

Helen was thirty years older than me. For a long time, we took care of each other and eventually Johanna and I took care of her for many months before she left this world. The sweetest death. Her long white hair combed out, her blue-veined hands folded on her chest, her last word the name of her son. I kissed her forehead and left the house and sank to my knees beneath the trees, leaving Johanna to wash her body while she grieved.

The most unfair thing in the world is that dogs do not live as long as we do. All these years later, I can hardly stand to think about that. He was with me as long as I could have hoped for, and then one day he lay down on the moss near my feet while we listened to the waterfall. He eased in as close to my leg as he could get. I ran my hand over his head, again and again, occasionally pausing to hold his silky ear between my palm and fingers, which always gained a little pleased groan from the back of his throat. I studied the tan speckles on his white legs, the graceful way his back legs crossed each other. I drew in the cedar scent of him. He looked up at me. I put my hand over his heart: faint, then fainter. His breath became thinner. He closed the watery eyes in his whitened face. He left me.

They are both gone from me, yes. The important thing is that they lived. They fought back. They were my true friends. They were my family.

ACKNOWLEDGMENTS

AUDREY MURPHY CAIN, Donavan Cain, and the Murphy family introduced me to the beauties of Sherkin Island, which was one of the first inspirations for this novel. The Sherkin Island Marine Station, run by the Murphy Family, and their guidebooks, were particularly rich resources. Robbie Murphy's pictures were a constant guide for me.

Mary McPartlan was one of the great singers and representatives of Ireland. She gave me the book *The Otherworld: Music and Song from Irish Tradition*, edited by Ríonach uí Ógáin and Tom Sherlock, which was particularly helpful to me. Mary passed away shortly after I finished this novel but lives on in its pages and in her music. Helen Gubbins introduced me to Glendalough on a perfect gray day. Her music, spirit, and friendship inform everything about this novel.

The character Helen McPartlan is named for and inspired by these two remarkable people.

I am thankful to the National University of Ireland, Galway's faculty, staff, and students, who were so welcoming to me during my time there. I am lucky to teach with colleagues and students at the Naslund-Mann Graduate School of Writing and at Berea College. Time spent at the Studios of Key West and Hindman Settlement School are essential to this novel's existence.

I am beyond grateful to Gavin Colton for his detailed guidance on cultural and colloquial details and his easy friendship. My thanks to Stephen McGann for answering political questions and for being my pal. Alice Hale Adams, Jane Hicks, Kevin Gardner, and Barbara Kingsolver were generous to read early drafts and to offer much-needed advice and encouragement. I'm grateful to my writing community. Booksellers, teachers, and librarians: thank you for all you do to get the written word into people's hands and to create community.

I am honored to work with people like Betsy Gleick, Michael McKenzie, Brunson Hoole, Lauren Moseley, and many others at Algonquin Books. Chief among them is my editor, Kathy Pories, who has made all of my novels so much better with her intelligence, expertise, and empathy. She's the best.

Every dog I have ever loved is contained in Seamus, but our beagle, Ari Prince Rogers Nelson, more than any other. Thank you to my children, Cheyenne and Levi, and my family, for everything. I could not get through the day without Jason Kyle Howard, much less write a novel. He is my Arlo, always.